# PSYCHO HUGE BEAST FROM OUTER SPACE

STORIES I FOUND IN THE CLOSET

Psycho Hose Beast From Outer Space

ISBN: 979-8-6476872-3-4

Published by Stories I Found in the Closet
www.cdgallantking.ca

Edited by Tamarind Hill Press
http://tamarindhillpress.co.uk/

"Stories I Found in the Closet" Logo by
Ann McDougall Design & Creative Services
www.facebook.com/AnnMcDougallDesign

Printed by Amazon
Available from Amazon.com and other retail outlets

For the boys from back home.

# PSYCHO HOSE BEAST FROM OUTER SPACE

C.D. Gallant-King

## PROLOGUE

*Pull Me Under*

November 18, 1929, 6:10pm

Kelly's Island, Burin Peninsula,

Dominion of Newfoundland

EJ Pratt wrote that it took the sea a thousand years to carve the face of a granite cliff, but only an hour to do the same to the face of a young woman. For Isaac Biddle, it took only a moment, and a single blood-curdling scream from his young wife, to age him a hundred years and make him crap his drawers.

Isaac listened to Mary's horrible cries from the kitchen, seated at the small table he had made himself, his hands trembling on a cup of tea. Biddle knew little about childbirth—he had seen cows and dogs delivered, sure, but no animal had ever sounded like that. It didn't seem natural. He had seen his cousin Maxim lose an arm to a sawmill's blade once; Max's screams as he watched his brothers slip and slide on a pool of blood while trying to recover their sibling's severed limb were the closest he could compare to the sounds Mary was making now.

His wife's sister, Juanita, emerged from the bedroom, and Isaac stood up. She was as pale as her white apron, which was smeared with crimson. Isaac felt weak and sat back down.

"It's not good," Juanita said, her voice tight.

"I'll go across the bay and get the doctor," Isaac responded, standing again. Going to find the doctor was good. It would give him something to do instead of just waiting around.

"You'll never make it in this storm."

"I've got to do something." Isaac was a man of action. Sitting here on his arse was like having rusty nails slowly driven into the fleshy part between his thumb and forefinger, a feeling he knew well as he had once gotten his hand caught just so on a gaff hook.

Juanita looked him dead in the eye, her grey eyes cold and unwavering. "Get the Benoit sisters."

Isaac recoiled as if his sister-in-law had slapped a maggoty haunch of rotting caribou meat on the kitchen table. "No. I will not have those witches in my house."

"Then Mary is going to die. I can't help her. You can't help her, and the doctor is too far away. But the Benoit sisters know things. They can save your wife and your baby."

The Benoit sisters were twins, offspring of an Indian hermit who lived somewhere in the mountains and a gypsy woman who had stowed aboard a French fishing ship and was abandoned on the rocks down near Harbour Breton. The girls had grown up in a godless home and learned magic tricks from both sides of their queer family. "God will damn us all if I let those heathen women into my home."

"Then I'll go get them," Juanita said, going for her coat hanging by the door. "I'm not going to sit here and watch my sister die. I'll risk going to hell to save her. You can sit in your misery and loneliness and feel righteous if you want to."

Isaac put up a hand to block the door. "Damn it woman, you're not giving me any choice."

"If you're a man, then no, you don't have a choice. You do what you have to do, to save your wife and child."

Questioning his manhood was the last straw. He should smack the woman upside the head for that slight. Isaac's own father had accused him of being unfit to be a husband, and Isaac had always vowed to prove him wrong. That had led him to numerous problems, like getting lost in the forest and chopping off three toes when he refused to ask for help cutting wood, or nearly drowning when he insisted on patching the hole in his boat himself. He had suffered grievous and unnecessary personal injury to prove himself a man, and this little shrew would not say otherwise.

Cursing under his breath, Isaac grabbed his own coat and pulled his wool cap down around his ears. "You take care of her until I get back."

"There's not much I can do." Juanita reached out and squeezed Isaac's arm, and he felt all the anger drain away. He fought back a sob that threatened to force its way up his throat like an angry squirrel. "Please hurry."

Isaac Biddle stepped out of the small, two-room house he shared with his wife into the worst storm the South Shore had seen in a lifetime. The rain was pounding so hard it was difficult to see. The sisters' home was less than a mile away, westward along the shore, atop a high cliff overlooking the Atlantic. Usually, it was a lovely stroll of no more than a few minutes, but tonight it felt like fighting through a crowd while being slapped in the face with a wet halibut. The raindrops fell so hard they actually hurt, and were surely leaving welts. He pressed on, relying on his innate sense of direction to lead his feet, hopefully not right off the bank into the crashing waves thirty feet below. He supposed that if he did fall to his death, at least he wouldn't have to deal with the witches.

He had no idea what time it was. The sky was so dark it looked like midnight, but Mary's labour had only started at breakfast time. It couldn't be more than late afternoon, could it? He felt disoriented, almost drunk, and wondered what the hell was even happening. A few days ago he had been so happy, excited to be a father. It wasn't supposed to go like this.

Under his breath, Isaac started to sing. He didn't know why. He didn't remember singing since he was a boy, and the men on his father's wharf taught him shanties and dirty limericks. In fact, the only time he ever remembered singing with certainty was the time he and his father had gotten caught in a bad storm out on the cape. He'd been so scared that his father told him to close his eyes and sing until they reached safety.

Maybe that's why he was singing now.

*Well oh, Lukey's boat is painted green,*

*Ha, me boys!*

Suddenly Isaac reached the sisters' door. They lived in a tiny home, even smaller than the one he and Mary shared. He saw light from under the shuttered windows so he knew that someone must be awake, whatever the time. Not that he wouldn't have awakened them anyway, but he hoped the hags would be less likely to put a hex on him if he didn't disturb them while they were asleep.

*Lukey's boat is painted green,*

*The prettiest boat you ever did see,*

*A-ha, me boys a-riddle-i-day!*

He pounded on the door but there was no reply. He pounded again to no effect. Despite the howling wind and rain, he was sure he heard someone inside—talking maybe? Singing? Yes, they were singing, he was sure of it. Were the women, like him, singing to distract themselves from the Armageddon-level storm threatening to blow their shack off the bank and into the Atlantic? That seemed plausible and would explain why they couldn't hear Isaac knocking. But what were they...

...were they singing the same song he was?

*Well I says "Lukey the blinds are down"*

*Ha, me boys!*

*I says "Lukey the blinds are down"*

*"Me wife is dead and she's underground"*

*A-ha, me boys a-riddle-i-day!*

Isaac felt the hairs on the back of his neck stiffen. What were the odds? No, it wasn't possible, he must have misheard. He convinced himself he had misheard, because he didn't want to think of the other possibilities. He pounded again, but there was still no answer, and the singing seemed to get louder. "To hell with this," Isaac thought, and in that moment made the fatal mistake of throwing the door open and stepping into their small porch.

Isaac knew something was wrong as soon as he opened the door for two reasons: First, the wind and rain suddenly stopped the moment the wood banged open. The world plunged into immediate and utter silence. Second, he saw the two Benoit sisters, kneeling stark naked on the floor, facing each other with a giant, slimy slug-like creature between them.

At first Isaac thought it was a seal, but it was red and bloody, like flayed flesh. Maybe it was a skinned animal? But he saw no features of any animal he recognized—no flippers, no paws, no tail, no eyes—just a huge mound of slimy, gruesome, pulsating flesh.

"Jesus, Mary and Joseph," Isaac breathed.

Both sisters' heads whipped toward Isaac, and what he saw in their eyes was a strange mix of absolute hatred and terror. Worse, their eyes were red and slitted like those of a cat.

"Get out!" they hissed in unison.

Isaac staggered backward away from the scene, out of the house. When he saw the slug-like creature rise up and throw itself on one of the young women, he turned and ran. She screamed as Isaac tripped and fell down the uneven front steps, smashing his knee on a rock. He howled and looked up, looking past the house and its occupants to the sea beyond.

Something was wrong.

The beach was too long, the waters receded farther than on the lowest of tides. The smell of dead fish and kelp and mud assaulted his nose, stronger than he'd ever remembered. Fish and crabs flopped on the rocks which had been exposed by the fleeing waves. How was this possible?

The water on the horizon looked much, much too high.

Isaac ran as fast as his bloody, throbbing knee would allow. His house was farther inland and on higher ground than the sisters' so it should be safe. He should warn the women, tell them to flee as well, but that was what you did with normal, god-fearing humans. What he had seen in that shack was not human, and not of this earth. Better the sea wash it away and leave the devil to sort it out.

The wave that crashed into the shore was taller than Isaac had ever seen, could ever have imagined. It was fifty feet tall, at least, and came up over the bank like the vengeful fist of God and smashed the Benoit sisters' house to splinters. In seconds, every trace of the witches, their home, and hundreds of tons of soil beneath were sucked out into the Atlantic. Despite his lack of empathy for the women, the sheer, brutal power of it made Isaac sick to his stomach. Sure, he knew to respect and fear the sea. Anyone who lived on this Island learned that from a young age. He had lost two uncles and a cousin to the unforgiving water, and had himself once watched a man, a fisherman from Marystown named Edward Reilly, die when his foot got tangled in an anchor line and was pulled overboard. Isaac had watched Edward struggle and drown, just a few feet below the surface, as other fishermen tried in vain to pull the snagged line back up. Isaac had watched the light leave Edward's eyes that day, and the memory of his last moments had haunted his sleep for years after.

But this, this was different. This was beyond the random chaos of a storm or a freak accident. This was the vengeful, unfathomable power of God and nature, joined together in an unstoppable, focussed force to destroy the Benoit sisters and whatever demonic evil they had summoned into this world. Man could never dream of standing against such power, and suddenly Isaac felt very small and insignificant. Nothing mattered. Not himself, not Edward Reilly or his wife Mary or his unborn child or the Benoit sisters. God and Nature were all-powerful, and they were nothing—nothing—to them, insignificant emmets that lived and died by the whims of forces unknown.

Isaac fell to his knees and began to recite the Lord's Prayer. He repeated it more times than he could count until his voice was hoarse and his injured knee screamed in agony. Tears poured down his face and he begged for the souls of his wife and child, who were both surely dead by now. He had failed, and nothing mattered. For a moment he considered throwing himself into the sea after the witches. Only the promise of damnation, and the thought of never seeing Mary and the baby in heaven, stayed his hand.

Finally, when his eyes had no moisture left, he rose and staggered back home. The walk seemed to take forever. What was the point? What was the point of anything? He knew what he would find, and he was in no rush to face it.

As he walked home, he passed his neighbours' houses. Some of them were gone, washed away by the same wave that destroyed the sisters' shack. Collateral damage was of no consequence when God set out to destroy those who had slighted Him.

Below the houses, the fishing stages and wharves were a state. Most were destroyed, as were at least a dozen boats, reduced to no more than floating splinters by the wave. People were screaming and sobbing, looking for loved ones in the wreckage-strewn water.

Isaac ignored them. He kept walking. None of it mattered.

When Isaac's small, clapboard house was in sight, the wind shifted and he heard a strange sound. At first he thought it was more crying from down by the shore, but this was different. This wasn't the wail of a woman, lamenting her lost husband, or a man, lamenting his crushed dory. This was the sound of a baby crying.

A baby crying in his own house.

Somehow, Isaac's eyes found tears again, and he picked up his pace as fast as he could manage. He thanked a merciless God for showing the tiniest bit of pity on these poor, miserable souls.

# CHAPTER ONE

*Friday I'm In Love*

August 20, 1992, 5:55pm

Gale Harbour, Province of Newfoundland

"Sonic the Hedgehog."

Pius adjusted his glasses and nodded, allowing no room for argument.

Niall snorted and gave him one anyway. "Are you mental? Super Mario is way better."

"As if. Mario's for little kids. Sonic is way cooler. It has more attitude for the modern generation."

Pius mashed some buttons on his controller and the small Asian girl on the screen in front of them did a spinning kick that sent Niall's big sumo wrestler flying.

"No fair!" howled Niall, throwing his controller on Pius' carpeted bedroom floor. "You cheated!"

Pius, despite being the same age as Niall, was a good head shorter, and was skinny as a rake. He did his best to look insulted, which was impossible with the rat tail hanging from his unkempt black hair. "How did I cheat?"

"I was distracted by your dumb opinions."

"Everyone knows the Sega Genesis is a better system. Better graphics, better sound..."

"How can you tell? Everything flies by so fast you can't even see what's going on!"

"Duh, it can move so fast because the graphics processor is better." Pius rolled his eyes as if it was the most obvious thing in the world.

Niall scoffed. "As if. It's boring. All you do is run. Mario has a dragon buddy that eats stuff and breathes fire!"

"Actually it's a dinosaur."

"That is beside the point!"

"That's it, let's switch to the Genesis and I'll show you how much better Sonic is."

"You mean put on Super Mario World? Sure, let's do that."

Pius sulked. "If you keep mocking me, I'm not going to let you come over here and play games with me anymore."

"Maybe your mom will play with me," Niall mocked. "Oh right, that was last night!"

There was a knock at the door. An instant later, without waiting for an answer, the door opened and Pius' mom walked into the bedroom.

Niall felt his cheeks burn hotter than that time he'd accidentally put his hand on a Coleman camp stove, and he started to feel sick. He heard Pius choke back a laugh so hard he nearly asphyxiated himself, and Niall made a mental note to punch his best friend in the nose at the first chance he got.

Pius' mom was hot. At least, Niall thought she was hot, in a high-waisted-jeans and big-hair sort of way. She was short and had blonde hair and blue eyes and looked nothing like her dark-haired son, Pius. He got his looks from his dad's side of the family, though the boy had gotten his diminutive height from his mother. Niall had had a crush on Mrs. Jeddore—Samantha—since the third grade, and Pius gave him no end of grief about it. Pius got excited looking at the women's underwear section of the Sears catalogue, though, so it was not like he could talk.

Fortunately, she didn't seem to have heard Niall's comment. "Hello, boys." She was dressed in shapeless pink nurse's scrubs. "I got called into work early so I won't be able to drop you off at your movie. You'll have to ride your bikes."

"Ah, mom," Pius groaned.

"Or you could stay home and not waste your money on a movie you've already seen ten times."

"Mom, it's *Batman Returns*. BATMAN. And I only saw it four times. Plus this is a one-night double feature of *Batman Returns* and *Cool World*. We can't miss this."

"It's okay, Mrs. Jeddore. We can ride our bikes. We're big boys."

Pius' mom smiled at Niall and Pius snorted back another laugh. Was that too much innuendo? Niall felt his face, which was surely already a deep shade of crimson, turn even redder. What was redder than red? Vermillion? That was a shade of red, right?

Fortunately, once again Mrs. Jeddore didn't seem to notice. "Thank you, Niall. I wish Pius was so mature."

Pius stopped smiling, and now it was Niall's turn to grin. Behind Samantha's back, Niall stuck out his tongue at his best friend. Niall would be the first to admit this was a little immature for a 12-year old, especially one who was trying to hit on his best friend's mom, but he still felt it was appropriate to the situation.

Niall usually prided himself on being grown-up for his age. He was taller than most of the boys in his class, and he kept his own dirty-blond hair neatly spiked like he had seen cool kids do. Well, like his older brother Nelson did, anyway. Plus he was into poetry (or at least told himself he was) and bands like Rush and Depeche Mode, which he also picked up from his older brother. But when it came to Pius (who's favourite musician was "Weird" Al Yankovic), his best friend since preschool, he couldn't help but be a bit childish at times.

"Oh, and your Uncle Dick is here, Pius," added Samantha as she left the room. "Harper too."

Harper was here? In this house? Mrs. Jeddore forgotten, Niall jumped to his feet from the edge of the bed, perhaps a bit too enthusiastically. He hoped Pius hadn't noticed.

"Ooh, Niall and Harper, sitting in a tree…"

He had noticed. So immature.

"C'mon, you dillwad." Niall dropped his SNES controller and strode down the hall to the rose-motif wall-papered kitchen, where Pius's dad Raymond was talking to Dick Jeddore, his brother. Technically they were half-brothers, but their looks must have come from their mother's side because the two men looked very much alike. Pius's dad just had a little more grey in his hair. Both were much darker than even Pius.

Dick's daughter Harper was sitting on a chair between the two men, staring off into nothing and twisting her jet-black hair between her fingers.

Niall had an inappropriate crush on Pius's mom, sure, and that substitute teacher they sometimes had for French class, and the girl who worked the Saturday morning shift at the Silver Scoops ice cream parlour, but his feelings for Harper were different. In comparison, his feelings for those other girls glowed with the heat of a candle (Samantha was maybe a gas barbeque), but his feelings for Harper burned with the heat of a thousand suns.

Harper was cute, though perhaps not in the traditional sense. She had big, round dark eyes and a round nose and was kinda rude, but Niall had crushed on her hard for the last two years, ever since he had seen her sing Sinead O'Connor's "Nothing Compares 2 U" at the elementary school talent show. It was perhaps a bit of an odd choice for a ten-year-old, but Harper was not a traditional girl and she had simply nailed it. By the end of her performance, both the vice-principal and the janitor were in tears. Now Harper was into Pearl Jam and Nirvana and dressed in oversized plaid shirts and baggy jeans, but Niall was okay with that, too. She was still the prettiest girl at St. Paul's Elementary in Niall's eyes.

Despite being his best friend's cousin, Harper also seemed completely oblivious that Niall even existed.

Niall was staring so hard at Harper that he hadn't noticed Pius's dad and uncle talking to him. Snapping out of his reverie, he looked at Dick Jeddore sheepishly. "What?"

"I said are you boys signing up for Boy Scouts this year?" Dick Jeddore was the local Boy Scout Troop master, as well as the local Fisheries and Wildlife officer. There was nobody who was more "in touch" with nature, and Harper had been brought up as a woodsy outdoors-type herself. Dick had been bugging Pius and Niall to sign up for Scouts for years.

"I dunno Uncle Dick," said Pius. "I'm going out for band this year and if I get in, I'm going to be spending most of my time working on my trumpet."

"I'm going to let that one slide," said Dick. "What about you, Niall?"

"I just don't want to."

The outdoors and Niall did not get along. He wasn't just allergic to bees and pollen, even the sight of birds and flowers gave him hives.

The fact that Harper had grown up as a woodsy camper caused him no end of existential dissonance. How could he be attracted to someone that different from him? It was like a blue-ass fly being attracted to an electrified bug swatter. Maybe it was the danger that thrilled him.

"He'd rather spend his time in his room by himself playing video games," said Harper. That stung. While absolutely true, something about the cruel way she said it cut Niall to the core. She might as well have said he was staying home playing with Pius' trumpet, too.

"I don't know where we went wrong," sighed Pius' dad. Dick patted him on the shoulder, commiserating. "Anyway, you wanted to borrow my hip waders. I'll go grab them from the shed..."

"Actually, hold on a minute." Dick was looking at a small black device on his belt. "Can I use your phone first? Just got a page from work."

"Of course, you know where it is."

Dick nodded and stepped out of the kitchen. Niall's dad grabbed his coat and boots to head out to the shed, leaving the three kids alone at the table.

After a long moment of awkward silence, Pius cleared his throat. "So, you excited about going back to school?" he asked his cousin.

"You don't have to try and pretend to like me," Harper replied. "Go back in your room and play Donkey Kong or whatever."

"Actually, we were playing Street Fighter II," said Pius. "And it's pretty cool, you can do these spinning heel kicks."

"And I like you," said Niall, a little more earnestly than he intended. "I mean, we like you."

Pius and Harper both turned to stare at Niall, and he tried to sink under the table. He only made it a few centimetres before realizing that only made him look more like an idiot, so he started to slide back up. Then he realized that probably looked really dumb, too, so he stopped in a weird, slouchy position in his chair.

"What are you doing?" asked Pius. "If you're trying to subtly scratch your butt you're doing a terrible job."

"Shut up, Pius."

Pius' dad and Dick came back into the room at nearly the exact same time. His dad held up a pair of high rubber boots, but Dick just shook his head. "Not going to need them after all. I just got called into work. With the weather warnings the Department's on high alert and they want all hands on deck, just in case."

"So our camping trip is cancelled?" Harper asked, sounding way more disappointed than Niall could ever imagine anyone being about a camping trip.

Dick put an arm around her. "Sorry, honey. We'll try again next week before school starts, okay?" A thought seemed to strike Dick, and his dark brow furrowed. "Shoot. I might be at work all weekend."

"So?" asked Harper.

"I can't leave you home by yourself."

"Dad, I'm twelve, I'll be fine."

Dick turned to his brother. "Ray, I hate to ask..."

Pius' dad smiled. It was a broad, friendly smile, that showed a warmth and sincerity that could not be faked. Pius smiled the same way. "Of course she can stay here as long as you need. The boys were going to the movie, she can go with them. They were going to see Spider-Man or something."

"Batman, dad." Pius often complained about how out of touch his dad was. He said he couldn't tell the difference between a Dennis the Menace cartoon strip and the X-Men. "It's Batman. And Mom said she couldn't give us a ride to the movie anymore."

"A ride?" Harper scoffed. "To the theatre? Why don't we just walk, or ride bikes?"

Behind Harper's back, Pius groaned. The smaller boy had the physical conditioning of a diabetic hamster; there was no way he was going to enjoy riding half-way across town to the movie theatre. Niall wanted to slap the pained look off his friend's pimply face. Any chance to spend some time with Harper was a chance Niall was going to take. Even if it meant riding across town in hurricane-force winds and torrential rain. "Of course we can ride. And of course, Harper is welcome to come with us. It's a double-bill with *Cool World*."

"*Cool World*?" Harper mused. "Sweet, then I'm definitely in."

Pius and Niall exchanged shocked looks, similar to the time they had walked in on Mrs. Grant, their 5th Grade Science teacher, making out with the janitor. "You know *Cool World*?" They asked in unison.

"Yeah, I love Ralph Bakshi. His *Lord of the Rings* movie was amazing; I wish they had made the second part. Plus, Brad Pitt is really hot."

Pius raised an eyebrow. Harper laughed, which was something Niall didn't think he had ever heard her do, at least not directed at someone besides himself. It was a glorious sound. "I'm just messing with you. He's a total fart-knocker."

## CHAPTER TWO

*Would?*

August 20, 7:45pm

It had started to rain. Dick Jeddore was parked in his official Fisheries & Wildlife truck at the edge of the old American military base overlooking the town water supply, sipping black coffee out of his Thermos and watching the water rivulets run down his windshield.

Gale Harbour had been little more than a backwater fishing town with a single dirt road before the US Air Force set up a base and airfield there during World War II. Newfoundland had been a strategic waypoint between North America and Europe during the war, and Gale Harbour's deep, protected natural harbour proved an excellent site for ships to supply Emery Hanson Air Force Base. The Base had provided the small town with a cultural and economic boom until it closed in the mid-sixties, and even now, over 25 years later, Gale Harbour remained a service hub for Western Newfoundland.

Dick remembered the Base when he was a boy, when there were still American servicemen all over town, and checkpoints with armed guards at the bridges. His first "job" had been delivering newspapers to the guards at the gates, which he stole from the box down by the post office. The servicemen paid him in cigarettes and stories about the girls they had left home, and the local girls they met in town. Many of them were older sisters of kids in Dick's class, and a few times he had gotten those girls in trouble when he passed those stories on to his friends, who in turn passed them on to their parents.

He had felt like a right little snitch for stooling on those girls at the time, but now as a parent to a young girl himself, he wished he had an 8-year-old to spy for him. His daughter Harper was at the Hanson Movie Theatre this very moment with two boys, and he hoped he had done the right thing leaving her with them. But Pius was his nephew, after all, and that Niall kid, though weird, was so awkward that Dick couldn't imagine he would even know what to do with a girl if she wasn't animated or wearing a superhero costume. It also helped that Harper could have beaten up both of them, probably at the same time.

No, he had a good kid, and though he felt bad cancelling their camping trip at the last minute, she knew how to take care of herself and would be fine. It was an unfortunate side effect of growing up with a single parent: Harper had learned at a young age how to be independent, but Dick wished that she hadn't had to.

Dick had a bad feeling. Something about the weather was throwing him off. Hurricane Andrew was only stirring up rain and mild winds in these parts, nothing like the damage it was causing down in the States, but there was still an odd feeling about this weather that put Dick on edge. Something about storms like this that caused people to do dumb things. It was why he'd been called in on short notice. Not just because someone was more likely to get lost in the woods on a night like this, but because someone was more likely to be out doing something stupid. Some people thought poaching game or fish would be easier on a stormy night because no one in their right mind would be out patrolling the rivers in this weather.

Dick Jeddore was not, strictly speaking, in his right mind.

It was why he was always drawn to the woods, to the rivers and lakes and bays. It was why he had become a Fisheries and Wildlife officer. He had an unnatural affinity and connection to nature. Sure, most guys his age had grown up fishing and hunting and could track a moose or gut a trout before they could ride a bike, but Dick took it a step further. He could track a moose with his eyes closed by scent and feel alone. He could sense when the weather was going to change, and could imitate the call of a hundred birds with ease. He was very closely attuned to the natural world around him, and tonight something felt very off.

A flicker of movement down by the edge of the water supply caught Dick's attention. It was probably just the wind and the rain. He hadn't actually come out here to patrol the lake on the edge of town, anyway. He had only stopped to finish his coffee before heading deeper off-road to check the favourite spots of local poachers. Most people would not have even noticed the unusual movement, but Dick Jeddore had unusual instincts, and he had long ago learned to trust them.

He hopped out of his truck, bundled in his raincoat and with a hat pulled down over his ears. Even in August, the rain was freezing cold, and the biting wind didn't help. He snapped on his flashlight and made his way down over the steep, rocky side of the bank, slipping only once. His eyes focussed on something dark sticking out of the water at the edge of the lake. He had seen something after all. Though it was probably just a fallen tree or a piece of garbage, he had to check to make sure. His gut was telling him that something wasn't right, and he was hoping and praying that for once, his instincts were wrong.

They weren't. Dick reached the water's edge, and his flashlight's beam fell upon a human foot, sticking up out of the black, churning lake. His insides turned to liquid ice. No, it couldn't be. He grabbed it by the ankle and knew immediately that it was. It felt like flesh and bone. Thin and frail, but definitely flesh and bone. And it was cold.

He pulled the body up onto the shore, revealing the pale, motionless form of a white-haired man in his seventies or early eighties, dressed in checkered green pyjamas. Dick choked back the bile that rose in his throat, but he forced himself to check the man's pulse and breathing. He had neither. Judging by his complexion and lack of body temperature, he had been dead for hours.

Dick had seen dead bodies before, but he had never found one himself, out in the open like this. Once, another wildlife officer had stumbled upon the corpse of a hunter who had accidentally shot himself and bled to death in the brush. He'd been dead for days before they found him, and picked over by animals. By the time Dick had seen the body, he'd been wrapped up and tagged, and the officer who'd found him had puked several times.

Dick didn't puke now, but he came close. As he climbed back up the bank, he distracted himself with questions. Who was the old man? How the hell did he get out here in his pyjamas and barefoot? He had heard of old folks with dementia wandering away from home, but they were a long way from populated areas. Usually his department was alerted to missing people, but there were no reports this time.

He managed to make it to the truck and called dispatch before he finally gave up and spilled his supper on the ground.

## CHAPTER THREE

*Fear (Of The Unknown)*

August 20, 11:25pm

"That was deadly!" Pius squealed as he came out of the theatre amidst a couple of dozen other pre-teens and older kids.

"You just like watching a guy have sex with a cartoon," Harper said.

Pius grinned. "I won't say I didn't not like it."

Niall had to admit he liked it himself, too, but he certainly wasn't going to admit it in front of Harper. The Hanson Movie Theatre, like most of the buildings in this part of town, had been part of the old military base, built for servicemen during and after World War II. Also like most of the other buildings on this end of town, it was rundown and hadn't been properly renovated in nearly fifty years. Its projector was dim and blurry and the sound system crackled and popped when it worked at all. There was a large stain in the middle of the screen that had never been cleaned, from when somehow had thrown a tub of buttery popcorn at it back in 1973 when they realized Roger Moore had replaced Sean Connery as James Bond in *Live and Lie Die*. Still, despite being old as dirt and reeking of mould, burnt popcorn and sweat, the theatre had been pretty full during the early showing of

*Batman Returns*, but it had cleared out considerably for *Cool World*. Part of that was people wanting to get home before the storm got too bad, but a bigger part was most people did not want to see a dude have sex with an animated Kim Basinger. Or at least they didn't want to admit wanting to see it.

The rain had mostly stopped by the time the late show got out a little after 11:00, so it looked like people took off early for nothing. Except of course, for that embarrassing sex with cartoons thing.

Someone who did not leave early was Brian Hawco, a weird little kid in Pius and Niall's grade who they never really hung out with, but he always seemed to be around. Most of the kids called him Skidmark, due to an unfortunate incident from kindergarten involving Brian's underwear. Kids were mean and had long memories. Niall was lucky (and very glad) that his own kindergarten incident, involving copious amounts of snot and his teacher's blouse, hadn't hung around to haunt him.

Skidmark, who despite being the same age as Niall and the others, was shorter than even Pius, but unfortunately weighed nearly as much as the other three put together. He sidled up to Niall, Pius and Harper in the lobby after the movie, his grey sweatpants stained with what was hopefully chocolate. "So what'd you think of that, guys? I mean, of course, *Batman* was better, but that *Cool World* was pretty sweet, too, don't you think? That was my third time seeing *Batman Returns*. Oh man, Michelle Pfeiffiffer is smokin' hot. Sorry Harper, don't mean to be sexist or anything, I mean she's also a very talented actress and I don't want to undermine her talent or anything, but even a blind man would have to acknowledge that she looks pretty fine wearing that leather outfit."

Harper didn't even have a chance to comment on Skidmark's rambling. She had barely opened her mouth before he continued. Niall wasn't sure if he was mispronouncing Michelle Pfeiffer's name on purpose or not.

"And what about Billie Dee Williams? I hear he's supposed to be Two-Face in the next movie. Wasn't he great in Star Wars? Lando is so cool. I can't wait until the next Batman movie. Do you think they'll make another Star Wars? Do you think they'll do a sequel to *Return of the Jedi* with Han and Leia's kids, or go back and do an origin story for Darth Vader? I hope Robin's in the next Batman movie, though I don't know how they'll make his stupid costume and elf shoes look cool."

Skidmark was having at least two conversations with himself, and none of the others could get a word in, not that they could follow close enough to make a cogent comment, anyway. Niall tried to end their misery. "Look, Brian, we need to get home before it starts to rain again..."

"My mom is supposed to be coming to pick me up. Do you want a ride? I'm sure she won't mind giving you a ride home, then you don't need to worry about getting wet. I can even call her to tell her you're coming, maybe that way she won't forget me this time. Did you bring jackets and boots?"

They were obviously wearing jackets and boots, but that was beside the point. "Skidmark, I mean, sorry, Brian," Harper looked embarrassed, but Brian was used to the nickname and didn't bat an eye. "Brian, we have our bikes, so I don't think your mom has room for all of them."

"No, you're probably right, but you can leave them here and we can come back with the truck in the morning. You should lock them up, though, if you have bike chains. There are some shady characters in this part of town. I heard a story about this guy whose cousin got the tires stolen off his bike out behind the Hanson Mall, only they weren't stolen 'cause he had actually wrecked his bike doing wheelies off the stairs over by the Heritage Centre and he didn't want to tell his mom what he did so he told his parents it was stolen. Oh look, Keith Doucette is behind you."

The three kids had been so focussed on ignoring Skidmark that his last comment didn't register until it was too late. When the dread reality of his words set in, the three turned as one to see the least desirable face at St. Paul's Elementary School in the crowd behind them. Niall couldn't have been more disturbed if Satan himself had shown up arm-and-arm with Hitler and Charles Manson.

If Skidmark was the smallest kid going into seventh grade at St. Paul's, then Keith Doucette was the biggest. It didn't help that he was also the oldest, having been held back a year in grade four. He was also the meanest, nastiest, and—whether by coincidence or not—the richest, and he was the biggest bully to awkward nerdy kids like Niall and Pius.

"Hey, pussies, what's up?" Keith was wearing a bright red Vuarnet t-shirt, denim dungarees and brand-new Air Jordans.

"We're just leaving," Niall said, ushering Pius and Harper to the door. Pius was actually trembling; he was nervous at the best of times, around Keith he was absolutely horrified.

"You watching your crappy Batman movie? You like watching a dude in a rubber suit punch other dudes?"

"Kinda," Pius stammered.

"Wanna find out what it's really like to be punched, Tonto?"

Harper, perhaps spurred by the racial slur, perhaps simply by her own righteous sense of justice, stepped between Keith and her cousin. Niall was impressed, he wouldn't have been able to do it himself. "If it's such a crappy movie, what are you doing here?"

"My girlfriend wanted to see it," Keith said, putting an unusually strong emphasis on "girlfriend." After he said it, he seemed to remember she existed and glanced around. "Where the hell did she go anyway?"

"Maybe she was just a cartoon and she got dipped in Judge Doom's turpentine?" said Brian Hawco. "That's a reference from a different move that combines live action with animation, by the way."

"Shut up, Skidmark." Keith shoved Brian hard, without warning. Brian slammed into the plexiglass case featuring the Coming Soon poster for *The Mighty Ducks*. Brian collapsed to the floor. The handful of other kids still in the lobby froze in horror.

Keith, ignoring the moans of the injured boy lying on the floor, went after his original targets. "At least I have a girlfriend and I'm not going to the movies with my cousin!"

"So what, barf breath?" Harper stood up to Keith, though he towered over her. "I bet you go to movies with your mom."

"Don't you dare talk about my mom," Keith growled. "If you think I won't hit a girl, you've got another thing coming, squaw."

Keith grabbed her by the collar of her army surplus jacket, and several of the assembled kids made gasping and "ooing" noises. Without thinking, surprising everyone including himself, Niall stepped in between Keith and Harper. Huh, apparently he could do it, after all. At least if there was a girl involved.

"Leave her alone, Keith," Niall said, with as much confidence as he could muster. He puffed out his chest and immediately felt stupid. Niall was tall, but he still had to look up at Keith, and the big gorilla snarled down at him. Niall could see the bits of popcorn stuck in the big kid's braces, and smell the cigarettes from when he snuck out to smoke during the movie.

"You wanna die, nerd?"

"Not particularly, no, but—" Niall didn't get to finish what he was sure would have been a sterling comeback. Keith cheap-shotted him with a punch right in the face, and Niall went down to his knees.

"What the hell is going on out here?"

The voice of authority came from the theatre manager, a weird old guy with crazy hair and a glass eye. He was well-known around town for the messages he left on the theatre's answering machine, where people could call and listen to his long, rambling synopsis and reviews of the currently-playing movies. On the phone, he was unintentionally hilarious, but in person, coming out of the dark theatre wielding a garbage bag and a flashlight, the stick-thin creature looked like a goblin emerging from his cave to challenge anyone who dared cross his domain.

Several of the moviegoers pointed at Keith and yelled "It was him!" and the bully immediately started going into his fake-remorseful voice. Niall felt hands grab him under the arms and pull him to his feet.

"Let's get out of here!" Pius hissed in his ear, and Niall didn't dream of arguing.

His jaw ached and he tasted blood in his mouth, but Niall got up and ran out the doors with Pius and Harper. "What are we doing?" she asked, following along. "The manager will deal with him."

"No, Keith will talk himself out of it, and then he'll come looking for us for getting him into trouble," Pius explained.

"That doesn't make sense!" said Harper.

"Nothing that idiot does makes sense!" Niall agreed. "But I've been punched in the face enough for one night."

"You didn't have to do that, you know." Harper was getting on her bike—a beat-up old red ten-speed that had seen far more use than either of the boys'—but she stopped and looked Niall in the eye. He froze and nearly dropped his own bike. "I don't think he really would have hit me."

"No, he really would have. He broke Suzie Fowlow's arm last year."

Harper recoiled in horror. "That was him? I thought she fell off the monkey bars. Didn't Keith have a crush on her?"

"He did," said Pius. "So you could imagine what he would do to someone he didn't like."

"That jerkwad. I should have punched him in the teeth."

"And then we'd still be peeling you off the walls of the Hanson Theatre. Come on, let's go!"

The trio finished mounting their bikes and peddled off into the night along the slick wet roads. The dark sky overhead threatened rain, and the wind still whipped about them in a frenzy. They were barely a hundred metres down the street when they heard a loud, high-pitched motor kick to life behind them.

"Ah crap," moaned Pius, already breathing hard from pedalling. "That's Keith's dirt bike."

"He rode his dirt bike to the movie theatre?" asked Harper, gliding effortlessly beside him.

"He thinks it makes him look cool," answered Niall.

"How did his girlfriend get here?"

"He probably made her walk," said Pius.

Harper spat. "He's a total buttwipe!"

Niall grinned. He adored this girl. "Yeah, you tell him that."

"We'll take Queen Street, and cut across the field behind the library," said Pius. "We can lose him that way."

Niall shook his head. "He knows where we live. He'll probably head straight to your house and just wait for us there."

"Then what do we do?" asked Pius. "We can't outrun him."

Harper smiled. "We don't go home. At least not right away. Come on, follow me."

The town of Gale Harbour, nestled in between mountains and the ocean, was mostly flat and devoid of trees. The buildings and houses were primarily small and functional, especially on this side of town that used to the military base. The going was pretty easy, which was good, because Niall and Pius were not particularly athletic boys. There also wasn't much cover to hide them from a determined bully, which is why Harper chose the zig-zagging route that she did.

They reached Queen Street, and Harper turned left instead of right, down past the mall and toward the middle school and the shoreline. She was very quickly pulling ahead of the two boys.

"How does she ride so fast?" gasped Pius.

"Come on, keep up," said Niall, increasing his own pace. His legs and lungs started to protest, but he wasn't going to let Harper see how much he was struggling. Sure, he would let Pius know later, and probably whine endlessly about his sore muscles, but now he was driven by something even stronger than the adrenaline of escaping Keith's wrath. He still couldn't believe he had stepped in front of Keith. His jaw hurt like hell and he was pretty sure the punch had knocked a tooth loose, but he had no regrets and would do it again in a heartbeat.

Well, maybe next time he would try to duck.

Harper rode past the turn-off for the school and down across the bridge that led to the beach. A road followed the shore a couple of kilometres to the fishing wharves and the harbour where the big ships docked across from the match factory, but thankfully she turned off the paved road onto the rocky shore only a few hundred metres away from the bridge. Niall wasn't sure how much longer he could keep up with her, and Pius was developing a concerning-sounding wheeze whenever he breathed.

"I think I'm dying," Pius gasped as he fell off his bike and onto the rocks just out of view of the road. "Leave me here. Let the crabs dispose of my body."

"You're such a wimp," Harper teased her cousin. She turned to Niall and suddenly concern flashed across her face. "Niall are you okay?"

Niall tried to massage the cramp out of his leg nonchalantly as if he were merely scratching his crotch. Come to think of it, he wasn't sure which was less embarrassing. His lungs were on fire but he did his best not to fall on the ground gasping like Pius. He prided himself on not being a jock, but he also didn't want to appear like a total wimp in front of Harper. "I'm good." The words sounded false even in Niall's own ears. They came through gritted teeth sounding like a man who was biting his tongue to keep from crying.

"No, your face! Your eye is getting all puffy."

He had been so busy just trying to get away, and then trying to breathe, Niall had forgotten the part where he'd been punched in the face. He reached up and gingerly touched his cheek, which sent shivers of pain through his skull. His skin felt like it belonged to someone else. Like someone who had just had their skin flattened by a cinder block.

"Ow," Niall whimpered. He was proud of himself for being so restrained. All he really wanted to do was cry.

"Jeez, he did a number on you." Pius was squinting at him from the ground, still not able to regain his feet. "You're going to have a wicked shiner tomorrow."

"I think he knocked a tooth loose, too." Niall felt around the inside of his mouth with his tongue. He realized the metallic blood taste he thought had been coming up from his lungs was actually coming from his gums.

Harper smiled. "Here I thought you were a weird artsy sissy. Turns out you're tougher than you look."

She punched Niall on the shoulder, and he did his very best not to wince. Her crooked smile gave him the strength to power through a hundred punches from a girl who was admittedly way stronger than him, and probably another swing or two from Keith, too. No more than two, though. A third would probably make him explode like a water balloon full of ground-up lasagna.

"Thank you?" Niall said. "I'm not sure if that was a compliment."

"You take it as one. A black eye will make you look cool."

Niall strongly disagreed with that statement, but he would wear clown shoes and a diaper on his head if Harper thought it would make him look cool.

"So now what?" Pius asked. "Do we make a raft and try to escape across the bay? I hear Cape-de-Cape is nice this time of year."

Harper rolled her eyes. "No, you doofus. We just sit and chill out for a while." She sat down next to Pius, facing the waves crashing on the rocks just a few metres away. "Watch the ocean. It's beautiful at night."

"It's cold," Pius said, putting his head back down on the smooth, sea-worn rocks beneath him.

Niall sat down on Harper's other side, an awkward distance away. Not so close as to be too intimate, but close enough that he was obviously still sitting beside her, instead of just at a random place at the beach. He could have reached out and touched her, but he did not dare to. He put his hands in his lap and tried to figure out what to say. The pain from his face and the stitch in his side were minor inconveniences, light years away from the terror of how to behave around a girl. It was cold, and he wondered if he should offer his grey windbreaker jacket to Harper, but she seemed unfazed by the icy gusts blowing off the Atlantic. She held her face up to the wind, wisps of black hair that had come loose from her braid blowing around her head. She closed her eyes and breathed deeply of the cool sea air.

On her other side, Pius choked. "Smells like rotting fish."

Niall had to agree with Harper. The sea was beautiful at night. Even with the wind and the damp air and the cold and the waft of dead fish, there was nowhere else in the world he would rather be. Except he suspected it was Harper he wanted to be next to, not necessarily the sea. But if next to a windy, soggy and freezing body of water was where she wanted to be, then that's where he would be, too.

The sky was dark with clouds, and they could only just make out the crest and crash of waves in the inky blackness. Distant street lights glowed yellow behind them, and across the bay on the opposite shore were the scattered lights of Cape-de-Cape. They were kinda pretty, and mysterious. In the dark, those lights could be anything, and not just the crappy old houses that Niall knew they were.

Between the air and the crash of the waves and the intoxicating knowledge that Harper was right there, just an arm's reach away, Niall started to become entranced. Despite getting punched in the face and having to ride his bike all over town, this was turning out to be a pretty great night. He knew he would have to go home soon, and part with Pius and Harper, but he hoped they could hold out just a little bit longer...

A deafening explosion and a flash of blinding light rocked Niall out of his daze. He nearly fell over as a wave of heat washed over him. The fine hair on his arms and the back of his neck stood up from his flesh. "What the hell? Was that... lightning?"

Pius, who had still been lying on the ground, scrambled to a sitting position. "That was awful close... was it right out over the water?"

Harper's gaze was transfixed on the waves. "I saw it. It was right there, just a few hundred metres offshore. But it came from the water and went up into the sky."

Niall was confused. "Does lightning do that?"

"No, it doesn't." Pius shook his head. "You have to be wrong. It happened so fast, and it was so bright, you must be wrong."

"I'm not! I know what I saw!"

A second flash and another roar split the night a moment later, and this time they all saw it. A huge, forking stroke of blue lightning shot straight up from the waves, about half a kilometre from where they sat, and disappeared into the cloudy sky above.

"Holy crap," Pius breathed.

"Did you see that?" Harper exclaimed, pointing frantically at the waves. "There was a boat out there! Where the lightning came from, the bolt started from the boat!"

Niall had seen it, but he couldn't believe it. It was a small fishing boat, and it had been engulfed in the blue glow of the lightning. "I saw it. Did the bolt destroy it?"

None of them could see anything, their vision full of spots from the searing brightness of the lightning bolt. Even after a few minutes, when their vision began to return to normal, there was nothing out there but black crashing waves.

"It's too dark." Harper paced back and forth as if she could get a better vantage point, but on the long flat shoreline, there was none. "I can't make it out."

She was right. They stared for a long time, but none of them ever saw another hint of the boat, and there were no further electrical discharges.

"So what do we do?" Pius asked.

"Nothing," Niall shrugged. He glanced at his watch, but the little digital numbers had disappeared. The battery must have died. Weird. "I've got to get home, it's gotta be almost midnight. And we're not even sure what we saw."

"I can ask my dad about it when he gets home tomorrow," said Harper. "Maybe there were more people who saw it? And maybe he knows more about upside-down lightning?"

"There's no such thing!" Pius repeated.

"Then what the hell did we just see, dillwad?" Harper pressed, pointing at the dark sky.

"I dunno. Aurora borealis?"

Niall wanted to tell her that he totally believed her and wanted to ask more about her opinions and thoughts on what it could have been, but in that moment the sky opened up and it began to pour rain. The wind picked up at the same time, whipping the raindrops at them sideways so that it felt like they were being pelted by a hail of water bullets.

"Let's get out of here!" Pius squealed, and the trio jumped back on their bikes and pedalled home. Between the wind and the rain and their exertion, there wasn't much chance to talk on the way, and Niall cursed his luck that his wonderful evening was ending so abruptly.

As they parted ways by the Smoke Shop convenience store – Pius lived a few streets further uptown from Niall – Pius yelled at Niall to call him in the morning. Niall would do better than that – he would be at Pius' door as soon as he had time to get dressed and eat a bowl of cereal. Not only was it the last weekend of the summer, but Harper was staying at Pius' place so she would still be there. When they went back to school, she would go back to ignoring him the same as always, but for now, he would use this opportunity to spend as much time with her as possible. And hang out with his best friend, of course.

When Niall got home, exhausted and wet, his dad was asleep on the couch and his mom was already gone to bed. He crept to his room, pulled off his wet clothes and collapsed on his bed. As he drifted off, he noticed the red glow of the numbers on his alarm clock said it was 3:35. That couldn't be possible. The movie got out at 11:00, the rides to and from the beach couldn't have taken more than twenty minutes each way, and they weren't by the water long. Niall had been practically counting the seconds he was with Harper. It shouldn't have been later than 12:30.

Niall was too tired to think about it. He was exhausted from riding home at full tilt. His clock must be wrong, he would fix it in the morning. He closed his eyes and fell asleep.

# CHAPTER FOUR

*Roll The Bones*

August 21, 1992, 8:15am

Dick's brown, rust-spotted pickup truck rolled to a stop in front of the Fisheries office, and he finished off the last dregs of the coffee at the bottom of his Thermos.

It has been a long night. He could have gone home after the incident with the body at the water supply, no one would have faulted him for that, but he didn't want to. Partly he knew there wasn't anyone to cover his shift, and he wanted to be out there in case anyone else was lost or hurt (poaching be damned at this point), but partly he also just wanted to be alone with his thoughts.

They couldn't I.D. the old man. He had nothing on him, and none of the handful of cops and emergency personnel who examined the body recognized him. He felt bad for the old fella, but more importantly, how did he get out there in the first place? Did he go out there on purpose? If so, why was he barefoot in only his pyjamas? Even if he was senile and got lost, how does a confused old-man walk three kilometres out of town, the first two of which are on a major road with plenty of witnesses, without anyone noticing? If he had wandered out of his house someone would have reported it by now, but the Royal Canadian Mounted Police had no missing person reports.

The other option, the one that bothered Dick the most, was that someone had brought him out there and left him on purpose. Whether he was alive or not before ending up in the lake was another unknown. The mounties and the coroner couldn't say for sure, and there were no obvious signs of foul play. In a small town on a weekend, it would be at least a couple of days before they got an autopsy, unless someone from the town or province put some pressure on to make it happen faster.

The rain had slacked off, leaving only a fine drizzle, but the wind was still biting cold. The Fisheries office was at a provincial government building in the part of town that used to be the USAF Base. Though the parking lot was mostly empty on a summer weekend and he parked as close as he could, the distance from the warmth of his truck to the front door of the building still seemed way too long this morning. Dick steeled himself to open his truck door and step out into the miserable weather, but then the radio on his dashboard crackled to life. He still had it tuned to the RCMP channel, and he heard the familiar, nasally voice of the local weekend dispatcher, Cheryl Murphy. "Any available units please respond to Port Hanson, down by Jake Cutler's wharf. Two bodies found, coroner's service has also been dispatched."

Two bodies? Three, total, in less than 24 hours? That was unheard of around here. Were they a result of the storm? Someone fell in the harbour, maybe? Cheryl didn't provide any details, and Dick wasn't technically authorized to be on this radio band, so he couldn't very well ask questions. It wasn't his jurisdiction, anyway. If they wanted Fisheries & Wildlife, someone would have let him know. He was also off duty; he should head home for a few hours of sleep, check on Harper, and then be back for the afternoon shift.

That's what he *should* do, anyway. But three deaths in Gale Harbour in one night was too unusual to ignore. And the old man's death still bothered him. It was unlikely there was any connection between the incidents... but what if there was?

Dick put the truck in reverse, backed out of the parking lot, and headed for Port Hanson.

No one gave Dick any trouble when he arrived at the crime scene. Fisheries and Wildlife often worked closely with the local RCMP, and they usually got along well. They shared the common bond that everyone else hated them—the RCMP for speeding tickets and Fisheries for poaching violations. Constable Burt Bennett, a rotund Mountie with a thick moustache who Dick sometimes played darts with, only nodded when Dick approached Jake Cutler's wharf.

Cutler himself, dressed in boots and oil slickers, was giving a statement to the Sergeant on the wharf. There were two fishing boats moored behind him, unusual for the small stage. One of the boats had a number of cops and medical crew crawling all over. Dick had flashbacks to the water supply the night before.

"Yeah, I was out early, same as I always do." Cutler took a drag off his damp cigarette. "I saw Mike Quinn's boat, just drifting out by Micmac Head. I knows he went out last night—told him not to, the weather was bad—but you know what Mike's like. I called out but got no answer, so I brought up alongside her and I could see two people lying face-down on the deck. I tied her up and climbed over and..."

Cutler's voice cut off. He was a sea-weathered, leather-faced old mariner, but Dick could see the hand holding his cigarette was shaking, and his eyes looked wet. "It was Mike and his brother Will.

They weren't breathing. I couldn't wake them up. So I radioed you guys and hauled his boat back here."

Mike Quinn was *dead*? And his brother Will. Dick had gone to school with Will. He didn't know him well, but he was a good man, always ready with a dirty joke and a wink. He had a wife and a couple of kids, too. His son was in Harper's class.

The Sergeant, a French woman from Quebec who had only recently been posted in Gale Harbour, put her hand on Cutler's shoulder. "I am so sorry. You were probably close to him."

"Quinn? Nah, Quinn was a right arse. Owed me money, too. His brother was a good hand, though. And it ain't right for anyone to die like that."

"Die like what?" Dick asked, and several heads turned to look at him. He felt out of place, dressed in his brown warden's uniform, but Cutler didn't bat an eye.

"Drown like that."

Dick raised an eyebrow. "Drown? I thought you found them on the boat?"

"Who are you?" asked the Sergeant. She was a short woman, with a strong jaw and broad shoulders. Her black hair was pulled back tightly, creating a severe angle to her pale face. The tone of her voice wasn't much softer.

"Dick Jeddore, Fisheries & Wildlife."

"Did you witness anything, Officer Jeddore? Because otherwise I don't see any jurisdiction you have here."

"Dick's a good guy," said Constable Bennett. "He helps us out a lot on cases in the bush. No one knows the backwoods around here better than Dick."

"Well," said the sergeant, not taking her eyes off Dick. She was studying him like a butcher deciding where to start cutting a low-quality slab of beef. "If we find out the Quinn brothers' boat somehow took a detour in the backwoods before ending up in open water, I'll be sure to ask Officer Jeddore for his input."

So, the new Sergeant had decided she didn't like him already, or at least people like him. He hated mounties who thought they were the be-all and end-all, and that they didn't need anyone else's help. He also knew there was no sense arguing with cops like her when they were in official business mode, so he decided to appeal to her human side. "Will Quinn is a buddy of mine, we go way back. Can you at least tell me how he died?"

The sergeant's thin lips tightened and Dick thought for a moment she was going to bare her teeth at him like a dog, but instead, she tossed her head and opened her notebook. "Looks like one of the brothers fell in and drowned, and the other tried to pull him out but must have taken in a lungful of water himself. There is no other visible cause of injury or potential cause of death. We'll know more when we get the coroner's report but it certainly looks like an unfortunate accident. I'm sorry for your loss, Officer Jeddore."

"Thank you, Sergeant...?"

"Tanguay," she replied, with a conciliatory smile. Was it supposed to be sympathetic? Condescending? Dick couldn't tell. "Marie-Ann Tanguay. Now if you excuse me, Officer Jeddore, if you would leave the investigation to the actual police?"

Dick bit his tongue, gave her an equally vague smile in return, and walked away. He tipped his cap at Bennett and headed back to his truck.

None of that made any sense. Sure, he could see one of them falling in, or both, or one of them going in after the other. But how the hell did they both end up back in the boat? How would one of them be strong enough to pull them both back on board, and then pass out? He didn't think Tanguay was lying that there was no other obvious cause of death. There had to be another explanation, one that wasn't so obvious.

Dick's thoughts couldn't help but drift back to the other mysterious dead body he'd found, barely twelve hours prior.

He started up the truck and radioed Cheryl, the RCMP dispatcher. It wasn't proper procedure by any means, and Sergeant Tanguay would have an aneurysm when she found out, but Dick figured he would take advantage of Cheryl's chatty nature before she ordered her to stop talking to the nosy Fisheries Officer. "Hey Cheryl, have you heard anything about the John Doe we fished out of the water supply?"

He didn't really expect that they had. It had only been a few hours, and on a Saturday morning no less. It would be ages before an autopsy could be performed. But for some reason he felt like he should just check...

Cheryl's voice crackled to life faster than he expected. "Yeah, we got a positive ID on him," she answered.

"Really? That fast?"

"Yup, someone was looking for him. Oh, and you're going to love this..."

## INTERMÈDE

*It had a long memory.*

*It remembered coming to this world a very long time ago, nearly four billion orbits around the primary. It was just a single, simple-celled organism back then, exiled from its own world as an abomination. As a mistake best forgotten and ignored. Alone and starving on this pitiful rock circling a young yellow star, it split itself and gave a portion of its being to bring something new to the primordial ooze of this infant planet:*

*Life.*

*It brought life to this world and watched as it grew and evolved. It also fed, never more than it needed, never more least it would destroy its food source. It also watched—watched its prey evolve from protobionts to bacteria to fungus to insects to animals to humans. The smarter and stronger they became, the smarter and stronger it had become, too. It evolved much faster than these pathetic life forms and often it had to wait for them to catch up.*

*Sometimes they did catch up, and they became too powerful. It had been forced to destroy civilizations that had grown too uppity more than once over the eons. It had destroyed them so fully that no trace or memory of them remained.*

But the last time, for the first time, it had failed. Ten thousand star cycles ago it had made its existence known and the humans met it and overcame it. One of their Hunters had figured out the trick to defeating it, and had buried it away for ten thousand turns of the seasons at the bottom of the ocean.

One hundred centuries was a blink for that which has lived for billions of years, but it was still pissed off. It spent the millennia plotting, seething, waiting, until a chance shift in the tectonic plates beneath the sea freed it from its prison.

It had not expected to find humans waiting to send it back.

It was getting really sick and tired of this world. It would have to wipe out these aggravating humans and start over again.

The second imprisonment was much shorter. And this time when it returned the humans weren't prepared.

Good. This should be easy.

# CHAPTER FIVE

*We Are Family*

August 21, 7:00am

    Niall's alarm went off and he rolled to a sitting position. It took him a moment to remember he was in his room, surrounded by posters of Geddy Lee, Michael Keaton and Psylocke. Why was his alarm going off? Wasn't it Saturday? Why in the hell would he have set an alarm for seven on a Saturday? And why was he so blasted tired?

    Then he remembered: Harper was at Pius' house.

    He jumped out of bed and yanked off his two-sizes too small Dick Tracy pyjamas, then grabbed some clean acid-washed jeans and his best Batman t-shirt out of the dresser. He rushed down to the kitchen and started shovelling Corn Pops into his mouth before he even had the milk in the bowl. He didn't even turn on the TV to check out Muppet Babies, which he would never admit to his friends that he still watched. It would be a re-run anyway. And he would be at Pius' in time to watch Captain N and the Super Mario Bros.

    Niall heard his mom in the bathroom as he was pulling on his sneakers. "I'm going to Pius'!" he called out, his hand on the doorknob. "See you later!"

    "You're not going anywhere!"

Niall froze at the sound of his mother's voice. What did he do? Was it because he was out late last night? Did she find out about something else he didn't even remember doing?

"What do you mean?" he called back. "Why can't I go?"

Niall's mom, dressed in a beige bathrobe, her head wrapped in a towel, appeared in the kitchen. "We're bringing your Nana to the nursing home today, remember?"

Dammit. He had completely forgotten.

Niall's mother gasped. She immediately went into overprotective mothering mode and swooped in. "What happened to your eye?"

Shoot. He had forgotten about that. But now that his mother was touching his face it ached like a hundred-kilogram Neanderthal had socked him in the side of the head. He didn't dare tell his mom, that, though. If he did, she would call Keith's mom, and Keith would get a mild talking-to that would set off his hair-trigger rage issues, and in the end, Niall would just get beaten up again. Probably much worse, too.

"Oh it's nothing," Niall lied. "Pius and I rode down past the beach last night on the way home and we were throwing rocks. He accidentally hit me in the eye."

His mom looked at him, crossly, her lips pursed in judgement. "Niall, we both know Pius throws like a three-year-old girl. He didn't do this."

Crap. His mom knew him too well. "Fine, it was Harper."

"She punched you?" she gasped. "Did you do something inappropriate?"

"What? No! She hit me with a rock!"

"Did you touch her?"

"Jeez mom, no, it was an accident. We were just goofing around." Niall felt bad lying, and even worse pinning it on Pius and Harper, but he was more afraid of what Keith would do to him than anything his mother might threaten. Not to mention she loved the Jeddore kids and would probably just blame Niall for getting himself hurt, anyway.

Niall's mother looked at him for a long moment, then smiled. "Okay, but you put some ice on that, alright? And if you have any questions about how and when it's okay to touch a girl, you ask me, okay? Don't ask your father."

"Mom..."

"Okay! Just get ready to go."

Right. Nana. "Why can't Nelson go with you?"

"Because he's working."

Right. His older brother usually worked weekends down at the drugstore, stocking shelves and pricing tampons and other embarrassing items.

"Why are you trying to get out of this? You wanted to go, remember?"

He did. Niall loved his Nana. As a child, he had spent many a morning with her before he started school, sitting on her lap or her couch reading stories and watching cartoons while his parents were at work. He still liked to visit her place for Sunday dinner and listen to her stories. Plus she always gave him fifty dollars cash for his birthdays and Christmas.

Of course, he hadn't spent much time there in the last few years, not since her mind started to go. She lived all alone, and she couldn't take care of herself anymore. That's why they were putting her in the nursing home. Niall had wanted to go with his mom and dad to drop her off, to help her get settled in. She had done so much for him, it seemed like a small thing he could do, even if she didn't remember him most of the time.

But that was before he had the opportunity to spend a whole day with Harper. He was torn between loyalty to a family member who helped raise him, and to his best friend's pretty cousin who, up to last night, thought no better of him than a stain on a pair of drawers.

It really wasn't much of a decision.

"Okay, bye mom, I'll visit Nana next weekend!"

"Niall…"

Twenty minutes later, Niall was in the backseat of the family Chevrolet, driving to his grandmother's house across town. As if they needed a reminder that Nana Josephine needed to go into the home, they found her in the living room, where she had unpacked most of the items Niall's mom and aunt had packed up the week before, and was taping up one of the boxes with her cat, Joey Smallwood, inside.

"I left him food and his litter box," Nana explained as her daughter, Niall's mom, led her into the kitchen while Niall and his dad retrieved poor Joey Smallwood from the box. The cat, very unimpressed by his adventure, scratched Niall and ran away to hide under the couch.

Nana Josephine was not that old, relatively speaking. She was only in her sixties, and from what Niall understood from overheard bits of conversation, it was very unusual for someone her age to be so far gone. And it had come on so fast, too. Niall remembered her, just a few years ago, vibrant and sharp-witted. Back then, she could quote EJ Pratt and no one could beat her at cards (Niall was fairly sure she cheated). Now she put the newspaper in the refrigerator and regularly baked shoes in the oven.

He was sitting in the backseat of the family car with Nana as the family drove over Micmac Head, a narrow road over a high mountain pass near the matchstick factory, that winded between alternating cliff faces and sheer drops. The nursing home was located on the other side, in the small town of Gale Crossing. Nana was staring at the window, watching the rocky mountainside rush by. On one of the rocks, someone had spray-painted something obscene about a girl named Karen, and Niall hoped his grandmother hadn't noticed it.

"How are the dogs, Archie?"

It took Niall a few moments to realize Nana was talking to him. "The dogs?" He had never owned a dog.

"You said they kept fighting." Nana was smiling. Her blue eyes were sparkling. "But I'm sure you found a way to keep them apart, didn't you, Archie?"

Archie was Niall's uncle, his mother's brother. Nana thought that Niall was her own son, instead of her grandson. At least that was better than the time she mistook him for an old boyfriend and told him she was looking forward to their wedding night.

"Yes, Nana." Niall didn't want to upset his grandmother by contradicting her. Sometimes she got upset when you pointed out that she was wrong.

Niall's mother didn't seem to have the same reservation. From the passenger seat, she called back: "Archie never had dogs."

"Of course he does, Phyllis. He has three dogs, a goat, two pigs and a horse named Blackie."

Niall's mom was named Barbara, not Phyllis. Niall didn't know anyone named Phyllis, as far as he remembered. And he certainly didn't think his Uncle Archie had all those animals - he was pretty sure his mom would have mentioned if they lived on a freakin' farm.

Niall's mother quickly confirmed his suspicion. "Mom, Archie didn't have any of those things."

"Of course he does," Nana replied, confidently folding her hands in her lap. "There's a cow, too, but that belongs to Benoit up the road."

"What is she talking about?" Niall's dad tried to ask his wife quietly, but he was always a terrible whisperer. Niall always found out what he was getting for Christmas weeks before Christmas morning.

"I have no idea," she replied, and Niall could see the concern on her face in the shape of lines across her forehead. "I don't know anyone named Benoit, and there was no one with cows back home."

Niall was curious. Nana must have been talking about someone she knew from her childhood unless she was completely making it up. They were now coming down the road on the other side of the Head, with the Atlantic on their right and the small, flat town of Gale Crossing on their left. They would be at the nursing home soon. He figured it wouldn't hurt to go along with Nana's delusions a little, to get to know a bit more about her. "Josephine, where did Benoit get that cow again?"

Nana's mouth curled at the corners and she tilted her head at him. "Across the bay in Marystown, Archie, you know that."

Marystown? Across the Bay? Marystown was on the South shore of Newfoundland, but Nana had grown up on the North shore, hundreds of kilometres away.

Niall caught his mother's eye and she looked as confused and concerned as he felt, but before either of them could say anything, Nana spoke again.

"And why are you calling me Josephine? That's not my name."

Niall was about to ask her what her name really was, but his mom was already saying "Of course it is, don't be silly. You are Josephine Whillet. You grew up in Lewisporte, remember?"

Nana looked confused for a moment and said nothing. She didn't look scared or angry that she couldn't remember, she just sort of *was*. Niall felt his own stomach tighten. No one spoke anymore until they reached the parking lot of Western Health Nursing Home a few minutes later.

The building was low and made of brown brick, and had a nice view of St. Stephen's Bay just across the road. Niall hoped his Nana had a room with a window so she could appreciate it, though he wasn't even sure if she would understand what she was seeing.

## CHAPTER SIX

*Life Is A Highway*

August 21, 9:30am

Pius hung up the beige plastic phone on its cradle on the kitchen counter. "Huh. No answer at Niall's house."

"So?" said Harper. She was eating a bowl of Cinnamon Toast Crunch cereal in her yellow pyjamas, an encyclopedia open on the table in front of her. "He's probably gone somewhere with his parents."

Pius shook his head. "He would have told me. He said he was coming over this morning!" Pius chose not to add that Niall would never have willingly turned down a chance to hang out with Harper Jeddore. He sat down at the dining room table himself and poured himself a bowl of cereal.

"So your dopey friend blew you off, so what? He seems like a bit of a fartknocker anyway. He tries way too hard to be cool."

"You think Niall is cool?"

"No, I said he *tries* to be cool. He fails spectacularly. He's an even bigger loser than you are. No offence."

It was debatable which of them was a bigger loser, but Pius understood Harper's sentiment. "No, that's fair. Winning the West

Coast Math Olympics three years in a row really doesn't count for anything, does it?"

"In junior high school cred? Only to lower it."

Pius was good at math. He liked numbers, they were predictable. Unlike people, who had things like emotions and personalities that were just confusing for him. Though he loved school and learning in general, he loathed the idea of starting Junior High School next week. Too many people there, and teenagers had more emotions than most.

Trying to forget about next week and the inevitable panic attack such a thought was going to bring, Pius focussed instead on what his cousin was doing. He adjusted his glasses and looked over her shoulder at the encyclopedia volume, which she must have taken from the den where she'd slept last night. "What are you looking at? Electricity?"

"I'm trying to find anything about lightning bolts that go backwards. Like, from the ground to the sky. There's nothing in here."

"Like last night? Maybe we just misunderstood what we saw. Maybe it was just like a normal lightning bolt? And we were wrong?"

"I know what I saw." Harper's voice was definitive and left no room for discussion. She often talked like that, which made Pius uncomfortable. That's why he liked hanging out with Niall, he was way more easy-going than most people.

Harper chewed another mouthful of cereal. "Hey, your dad works for Light & Power, right?"

"So?"

"Then he should be an expert on electricity, right. Let's ask him."

"Uhh." Pius didn't like the sound of that.

"What's wrong?"

"If we ask him about it, he'll ask why we're asking. We can't tell him we were hanging out down at the beach at midnight in the middle of a hurricane. He'll flip."

Harper snorted. "So just tell him we saw it on TV or something."

Pius guessed that would be okay, but he was still uneasy about it. He was terrified of what his parents would do if they found out what he did last night. They might take his Sega Genesis. Not every parent was as cool as Uncle Dick about their kids wandering all over the place without permission. "He's at work, anyway. Mom said she saw him before he left and he was supposed to be busy all day. There's a lot of power lines down from the storm."

Harper got up from the table and slammed the Encyclopedia closed. "So let's go find him. Do you have anything better to do?"

"Well, I was going to wait for Niall to come over so we could play *Final Fantasy 2*. We were going to go after Baron..."

Harper rolled her eyes so hard she could have been one of the pretty girls who always shot Niall down when he asked them out. There was a certain look all girls seemed to have mastered to show you how disgusted they were with a boy. Even being a tomboy, Harper seemed to have the gene. "Look, Pius, you always go on about games and adventures and stuff. Why don't you go on a real adventure for once?"

Pius thought about that, trying to come up with an excuse. He didn't think she would accept because he had outgrown his rubber boots and didn't want to get his feet wet. Instead, he went with: "I can't go anywhere without telling my mom."

"So go tell her."

"She's asleep! She worked the night shift last night!" It was the only reason she didn't freak out when they came home at three in the morning... which was way later than Pius had imagined it could have been, so he was glad his dad was passed-out and his mom wasn't home when they got in.

Harper's face lit up. "You said she spoke to your dad when she got in, right? Maybe she knows where he is." Harper spun on her heel and headed down the hall toward the back of the house.

"Harper? Where are you going?" Pius realized what his cousin was doing and his heart plummeted into feet. He thought he was going to puke. "Don't wake up my mom!" he hissed.

Too late. he heard the click of his parents' bedroom door, then a few moments later she heard a crash. The door closed and Harper came out a second later.

Pius' heart was racing, but Harper was unperturbed. "She said your dad was supposed to start working in Keeping first. He should still be there for a while."

"What was that crash?"

"She threw a slipper at me. I ducked and it smashed into one of your baby pictures. Oh, and she said it's okay if we leave the house for the day."

"Really?"

Harper shrugged. "Well, her exact words were something along the lines of 'get the frig out of my house,' but it means basically the same thing."

Keeping was another small town that shared a border with Gale Harbour, ostensibly part of the same community but technically its own municipality, like a suburb of Gale Harbour. This was hilarious as the population of Gale Harbour itself was only marginally higher than a single big high-rise on the mainland, so saying it had a "suburb" was a bit of a joke. Plus, people who actually lived in Keeping hated when you called it that.

It wasn't a long trek by bike, even along the wet and muddy street, and they crossed the single bridge into Keeping less than twenty minutes later. As usual, Harper wasn't breaking a sweat while Pius was gasping for air.

Pius' dad was easy enough to find. Keeping wasn't that big, and after riding up and down only a few narrow, tree-lined streets they found the two big red Light & Power trucks parked alongside a busted power line, knocked down by a large fallen birch. The tree's large trunk and branches had already been pulled away, and someone was up in the lift bucket of one of the trucks, doing some work on the pole itself. Pius saw his dad on the ground in overalls, an orange safety vest and a yellow hard-hat.

"Pius?" asked Raymond Jeddore. "What are you doing out here? Is something wrong?"

"I just came out... for a bike ride..." Pius managed between gasping breaths.

"You're not exactly known for your bike riding expertise," his dad said, and the black-mustachioed man in identical coveralls beside him chuckled. "That's why I was concerned."

"Actually, Uncle Ray," Harper blurted out. "We had a question about electricity."

"Um, okay." Pius' dad looked at his fellow utility operator and shrugged.

"Actually it's about lightning. Is there such a thing as lightning that goes in reverse? Like, from the ground to the sky?"

Both men looked puzzled. "No, I don't think so. Why?"

Harper's plaid-jacketed shoulders fell. "No reason. Just something we saw on TV."

"Well, you can't believe everything you see on TV," said Mr. Jeddore.

"Actually, lightning does travel from the ground up," said a voice above their heads.

Pius, Harper and both men turned to look up at the lift bucket, which was now slowly lowering back down toward the earth. Inside was a young woman in a yellow hardhat, orange safety vest and goggles.

"Excuse me?" asked Pius' dad.

"Just let me get down and I'll explain," said the woman. "This thing freaks me out."

She was indeed clutching onto the sides of the yellow bucket like it was a life-raft in the Atlantic, and when she finally climbed out and down to the ground, her hands and legs were visibly shaking. She removed her safety goggles and wiped wisps of sweaty blonde hair from her freckled face. She took a moment to compose herself, and Pius couldn't blame her. Being up that high would have terrified him as well. He got woozy just climbing to the top of the slide at the Lions Club playground. "Lightning is caused by electrons flowing through the atmosphere from highly-negatively charged clouds to the positive-charged ground," explained the woman. She produced a rag from her coveralls and wiped her forehead. "The electrons can also flow back in the opposite direction, especially from very tall structures like a radio tower. In fact, because the air is already ionized from the cloud-to-ground strike, the return ground-to-cloud stroke is often faster and brighter."

Harper and the two men seemed lost, but it made perfect sense to Pius. "Of course. I would imagine that it happens all the time, then."

"Pretty much," the woman agreed. "It happens so quickly though, you can't really see it with the naked eye. It just looks like one big lightning bolt. Scientists have speculated about the existence of ground-to-cloud lightning for a hundred years, but we've only just begun to create cameras fast enough to prove it."

Pius' dad cleared his throat. "Yeah, this is Jenny. She's new, she just finished an electrical engineering degree up on the mainland."

"That's so cool," said Harper.

Pius was confused, as if someone had just tried to tell him that you cooked food in the refrigerator and the stove was used to chill your popsicles. His dad made it sound like there was something wrong with studying up "on the mainland," meaning mainland Canada, off the island of Newfoundland. "Dad, don't you have a degree in some kind of science?"

Mr. Jeddore cleared his throat again, and his friend slapped him on the back. "Are you kidding? Your dad just barely knows which wires to connect so as not to electrocute himself. Your dad and me, we got grandfathered in from back in the day when you didn't need a fancy degree to work for Light & Power. You just needed some work boots and some safety gloves, and even the gloves were optional."

Pius didn't know what to say. His dad has always seemed so smart to him and had always encouraged him to study hard and get a good education. Pius knew his dad wasn't a scientist, but he was still in charge of a lot of high-tech equipment and making sure the power was working for thousands of people on the West coast of Newfoundland. It was an important job, but he didn't even have a university degree?

His dad must have seen the confusion and disappointment in his face, but just as he started to open his mouth to say something, Harper butted in, "But does the lightning ever just come out of nowhere, without a cloud-down strike first? From say, the middle of the ocean or something straight up into the sky?"

Jenny wrinkled her freckled, sweat-glistened brow for a moment, but then shook her head. "I don't think so. Nothing that's ever been documented or studied, anyway."

"Right. Well, thank you."

Harper had to pull Pius away from the work crew. He was completely at a loss, and didn't know what to do. He knew his dad still worked hard and provided for his family, but Pius couldn't help to lose a little bit of respect for him. School was so important. How had his dad tricked the system into getting by without having a proper education?

"So what the heck did we see?" Harper asked him as they rode away.

It took Pius a moment to snap out of it and hear what she had asked. What indeed? Man, his whole world was turning upside down.

# CHAPTER SEVEN

*Poison Heart*

August 21, 10:10am

"Your mother will be perfectly comfortable here," said the pleasant young nurse in peach-coloured scrubs, leading the family down the halls of the nursing home. She had a cute face and pretty brown eyes, but Niall was so weirded out by the smells and sounds of the place that he barely even noticed. He did notice, of course, he just didn't obsess about it as much as he usually did.

Niall was pushing Nana Josephine in a wheelchair, which she didn't usually need. She had been so lost and unresponsive when they got out of the car that the staff had insisted it was probably in her best interest.

It looked mostly like a hospital to Niall, though a passing attempt had been made to make it look more "homey." He supposed that's where the name Nursing "Home" came from. There were a couple of potted plants, a few classic Newfoundland paintings on the walls—Niall recognized a print of Ann Harvey saving survivors of the shipwreck *Despatch* that he'd seen at least three other times, one of which was in a pizza parlour. People around here seemed to love scenes of the ocean wrecking stuff, even while they were eating donairs and garlic fingers.

"She will have 24-hour monitoring," the nurse went on, "as well as care from top-notch, professional staff. We have regular social events in the lounge like music, bingo, card games, plus plenty of time to catch up with old friends and make some new ones. You're from Lewisporte, aren't you Mrs. Whillet?"

Nana said nothing. After a moment of awkward silence, Niall answered for her. "She grew up there, yes. Didn't you, Nana?"

The nurse, a short woman with light-coloured hair pulled back in a tight bun, didn't wait for the old woman to respond. "We've got a couple of people here from Lewisporte. You may know some of them. There's Edward Tobin, he was a fisherman, and Suzanne MacDonald, I think she worked in the Anglican parish."

Still nothing. Finally, Niall's mother said, "She's been feeling a bit off today. Probably all the disruption of moving to a new place."

The nurse shook her head sadly but was incongruously smiling. "Of course. Would you like to rest, Mrs. Whillet? We'll take you to your room."

A few minutes later they arrived at a simple, plain room with a bed, dresser, and chair. "You can spruce it up with your own pictures and articles from home, of course," the nurse went on. "But I'm sure you'll find it comfortable. All of our residents do."

There was a strange noise from the room across the hall, and all eyes turned to the open door. Inside was a well-decorated room of a woman who had obviously lived there awhile. She had pictures of family members, a homemade knitted quilt on her bed, doilies on everything. Sitting on the bed, on top of the covers, was a tall, frail woman. She looked much older than Nana Josephine but it was hard to be certain; she was so thin she looked like a skeleton, and her eyes were sunken and dark.

"That's your neighbour, Ms. Kane," the nurse said in a cheerful voice. "She doesn't say much, so I'm sure she won't bother..."

"What are you doing here?" Ms. Kane demanded. Her voice was so harsh and sudden that Niall, and most of the adults, jumped. She had a strange accent, and it sounded oddly to Niall like a cross between a stereotypical backwater "Newfie" accent and Apu from The Simpsons.

"Ms. Kane," said the nurse, after taking a second to recover from her surprise. "That's not a nice way to speak to your new neighbour. This is Mrs. Josephine Whillet."

"My sister." The frail woman wasn't looking at anyone. Her gaze seemed to be staring a hole into the wall.

"Excuse me?" asked Niall's mom.

"My sister came to visit me last night."

Niall's family looked to the Nurse for clarification, but she seemed just as shaken as when Ms. Kane had spoken abruptly the first time. "I'm sorry," she said to Niall's mother. "She's usually very quiet. I'm not sure what's come over her. Unfortunately, with residents getting up in age as many of ours are, we do occasionally see sudden changes in..."

"My sister came to visit me last night!"

Ms. Kane came off the bed with a speed and ferocity that terrified Niall. He instinctively stepped back, away from Nana's chair, and the older woman crossed her room and the hall far faster than any 90-year old woman should have been able to. She shoved Niall's dad aside and wrapped her long, boney fingers around Nana's throat.

Nana gasped, not even having time to scream before the pressure closed on her airway. The nurse was on her, pulling her away only a split-second faster than Niall, who grabbed the old woman's other arm. Niall was shocked by her strength. Despite looking as frail and thin as a Vienna sausage, her arms were as stiff as metal rods. Between the two of them, they yanked Ms. Kane off of Nana, who was white with shock, her eyes bulging in her face. The nurse was calling for help and within seconds, more staff appeared and helped drag Ms. Kane back into her room.

The nurse was desperately apologizing as they wheeled Nana into her own room. His mother was fawning over Nana and his father was flustered, probably embarrassed that a woman fifty years older than him and forty kilograms lighter had just flattened him like Bob Probert with a cross-check. A moment later, both doors closed and Niall was left standing alone in the quiet hall.

He considered going into Nana's room but it was already crowded and he didn't really want to see her like this anyway. He didn't want any part of this. He was already uncomfortable with his beloved grandmother going into this place, and the last few minutes did nothing to make him feel any better about it. He needed air, and he needed time to think.

Niall headed back the way he thought led to the front door. He wasn't sure if he was just going to go outside or maybe go wait in the car, but he had to get out of this place. This was worse than when Pius beat him at *Street Fighter*. This was real life.

As he approached the nurses' station closest to the front door, Niall heard a familiar voice. Dick Jeddore? Harper's dad? Did they have a relative here? He didn't think so, at least not on Pius' side of the family. He couldn't see Dick Jeddore yet, but his voice was unmistakable. Niall was about to round a corner and say hi, but something the man said made him stop in his tracks.

"Can you please tell me anything about the deceased?"

Deceased? Who had died? And why was Dick Jeddore—a Fisheries and Wildlife officer—asking about it?

Niall paused to listen, standing back just shy from the view of the desk, pressed against the ugly pastel wallpaper.

He heard the nurse respond, "I'm sorry, sir, I already answered all of the police's questions. I'm not supposed to share details about any of our residents."

"I know, but I'm the one who found the body. It kept me up all night thinking about it. Look, Gladys, you're married to Nolan Swyers, right? Me and Nolan go way back. We used to go fishing up behind Barachois, did he ever tell you that?"

"Yes, Dick, I know about..."

"Did he ever tell you about the time he got drunk and fell in the brook, nearly got frost bite on all his toes and probably would have lost a foot if I hadn't dragged him back to camp and held his feet until they warmed up? Or when he stabbed himself with a hunting knife and I had to carry him back to town with the thing sticking out of his hand?"

"He still has the scar."

"Went straight through, right between his middle and ring finger. He got so much blood all over my truck."

"So Nolan is an idiot, what's your point?"

"Please Gladys. Please do me this little favour."

Even from his hiding place, Niall could hear the nurse sigh. "Okay, fine," she said. "His name was Robert Hulan. Seventy-eight years old, from Robinsons. His daughter comes by with her family a couple of times a year. He wandered out of here yesterday afternoon during the storm. By the time we noticed and sent out people to look, there wasn't hide nor hair of him."

"Yesterday afternoon?" By the tone of Dick's voice, Niall could tell he didn't believe the woman. "Come off it. You just said that to the mounties so as not to make yourselves look bad for losing the old man for what, twenty-four hours? More?"

"No, I'm serious. He was here for dinner yesterday at noon, everyone saw him."

There was a pause. "Does he drive?"

"No. He's blind."

"Jesus, Mary and Joseph, Gladys, I found him at the Gale Harbour water supply at eleven last night. How in the hell does a seventy-year-old blind man walk twenty kilometres, over Micmac Head, in the middle of a storm?"

"It's not twenty kilometres... The cops didn't seem concerned."

"Someone must have picked him up."

"It was just an accident."

Niall was so focussed on the conversation around the corner that he didn't see another woman approaching him from behind. He nearly jumped out of his skin when she stopped and asked, "Are you waiting for someone, son?"

"No, I... I'm just on my way out to the car. My grandma is here."

Niall had accidentally stepped away from the wall, and now the nurse's station and Mr. Jeddore were in full view. No way to hide and pretend anymore.

"Hi, Mr. Jeddore."

Dick looked startled. He also looked incredibly ragged and tired. He had bags under his eyes and a dark shadow of unshaven stubble across his face. "Niall. What are you doing here?"

"We're dropping off my Nana. She's moving in, I mean, we're putting her in... How's Harper?"

Dick seemed to be put off-balance by that question. "I... haven't spoken to her actually. I haven't been home yet, she's still at Pius' house."

"Right, of course."

"You guys have fun last night?"

Fun? What did he mean by that? "Excuse me?"

"At the movie? You know. Batman. Bam. Kappow. Batarangs and Bat-Shark Repellent."

Niall felt embarrassed for Mr. Jeddore, but he didn't say anything. Why did old people even try? "Oh, yeah, it was great. Look, I gotta go get something from the car..."

"Yeah, sure, no problem. I'll tell Harper you said hi. Oh, and Niall..."

Niall stopped halfway to the door and turned back.

"I'm sure they'll take good care of your grandmother here."

Niall caught a look between Mr. Jeddore and Gladys that he wasn't supposed to see or understand. It was an angry look—Mr. Jeddore was mad about what had happened to this Robert Hulan guy, and Gladys was mad that she—or at least the place she worked for— was being blamed for it.

Niall just nodded and hurried out. He didn't want to think about his Nana in this place anyway, and now he had to worry about her wandering out and getting lost and killed? This was turning out to be a terrible day. He really wished he had stayed home with Harper and Pius. As he walked outside, he noticed that the sky had turned very dark. A few moments later, the rain began to pick up once again, and Niall discovered the car doors were locked.

## CHAPTER EIGHT

*Everything About You*

August 21, 10:30am

"Can we..." Pius gasped as they pedalled down the Harmon Highway, a main access road bordered by the town on one side and mostly woodlands on the other. "...can we take a break?"

Harper looked at him, disgusted. She did that a lot. "A break? We've only been riding for 10 minutes. Plus, it's pouring rain."

"Yeah... but most of it... was uphill."

With an exasperated sigh, Harper pulled over on the dirt shoulder of the road. Pius pulled up next to her, wheezing. "Just... need a minute."

"You need to exercise more. You're going to have a heart attack before you're twenty, Pius."

"I don't need to exercise to do calculus. And I'm fine... can we just go a little slower? My legs are still sore from last night."

"My god, you're so lame. Fine, we can slow down... Oh, no."

Pius was looking at his shoes and trying not to puke. "Oh no, what?"

"Your friend's here."

Pius looked up to see Keith Doucette riding toward them on an 18-speed bike that probably cost more than his dad's car. To be fair, the car was twenty years old and was held together with wire and duct tape (of course it was, his dad didn't even go to university, how was he supposed to afford anything better?), but Keith's bike was still pretty sweet.

"Ah, man. I can't run away today. Please don't do anything to piss him off."

"Hey dirt bag!" Harper called out. "What happened to your dirt bike?"

Pius felt anger and fear shoot through his body in equal amounts. He had no idea what to make of it. "Harper!" he hissed through gritted teeth. "What are you doing?"

Keith pulled up in front of the cousins. He was so big close up, he looked almost ridiculous on a bicycle. His buzz cut was so sharp you could grate cheese on his head. A random truck drove past on the Harmon Highway, its engine the only sound besides Pius' heart trying to hammer its way out of his chest. "Well, if it ain't a couple of jackytars. Where's your boyfriend with the glass jaw?"

"He's not my boyfriend," said Harper.

"I wasn't talking to you." Keith was staring at Pius with a wicked, evil look in his glassy blue eyes. Pius had seen that look before, on the neighbour's dog just before it killed and shredded a stray cat that had wandered into its yard. "I've got a bone to pick with your boyfriend, Tonto."

"Talk to the hand, jerkwad." Harper tried to shoulder in between Pius and Keith, but Keith just kept pushing forward to get in Pius' face, despite the much smaller boy's continued efforts to back away from him.

"I lost my dirt bike because of Niall." Keith was smiling, showing perfect white teeth, but his voice was seething with hatred and anger.

"What?" Pius blurted out. "Did he steal it?"

"The theatre manager called my parents and my dad took it away."

"Well, duh. You did punch Niall in the face," said Harper.

Keith turned to Harper and growled. "My dad took my dirt bike because I got caught and he was embarrassed to be called out by the stupid scummy manager at the theatre. He told me I should have beaten the shit out of Niall out back where no one could see."

Great. Nice to see adults being the voice of reason. "I don't know where Niall is," Pius said, his voice soft and scratchy in his throat. "I'll let him know you're looking for him."

"Tell him I'm going to kill him. Murder him. And, in the meantime, maybe I'll give you another message you can pass on..."

Keith raised his fist to swing. Pius flinched and Harper tried to grab the big boy's arm, but Pius knew it was no use. Keith was going to cave in his face, and if he survived, all he could do would be to warn his best friend that he was next.

A car pulled up beside the trio: an Royal Canadian Mounted Police cruiser. Keith stopped mid-punch, his fist cocked back and Harper hanging off his elbow. Pius was cowering with his hands over his head.

A police woman behind the wheel leaned over to talk to them through the passenger window. She spoke with a French accent. "What's going on here?"

"Nothing officer," Pius squeaked. Before he knew what happened Harper grabbed him and pulled him back toward his bike.

"Keith here was just calling cops dirty pigs and we were standing up for the brave men and women who protect our community." Harper threw the accusation out while holding her bike between them. Keith looked around confused, then focused on the police officer, who was staring at him angrily.

"No, I didn't!" Keith protested, hands raised.

"Were you about to hit that boy?" she asked.

Keith didn't answer. He just gave Pius the finger and jumped onto his own his bike. The cop yelled at him but made no sign of trying to stop him. On his 18-speed he was gone in seconds.

"Aren't you going to do something?" Harper demanded.

"What am I supposed to do? Arrest him for being a bully?" The officer sighed. "You kids okay?"

"Yeah, thanks," mumbled Pius. He knew they were only delaying the inevitable. One of these days Keith was going to get his hands on him or Niall and it was going to end very badly. The dread sat in the pit of his stomach like acid.

The officer offered a smile. She was pretty, in a stern way. Niall would probably like her. "Don't worry, jerks like that never amount to anything."

"Actually," said Harper. "My dad says they grow up to be managers and politicians."

"You are way too cynical, young lady." The cop nodded in agreement. "Your dad is not wrong, though."

While Pius was wondering if a police officer needed a university degree, the radio on the car's dashboard, below what appeared to be baby shoes hanging from the rear-view mirror, crackled to life. The cop excused herself and picked up the radio receiver. "Go for Tanguay."

"Sarge, we found another body."

Pius heard himself gasp. The officer glanced at him and Harper and turned the volume on her radio down.

"Where?" she replied into the microphone. The reply came back muffled and indistinct. "*Tabernouche*. Ten-four, I'm on my way."

Sergeant Tanguay put the car in gear and nodded to the kids. "You kids keep out of trouble okay? And stay away from that asshole."

They didn't even have time to answer before she peeled away, sending up a cloud of mud and gravel before doing a U-turn in the middle of the road and zipping away with her lights and siren blaring.

"Wow," said Harper.

"Yeah," agreed Pius.

"Let's go check it out." She started to get back on her bike.

"What? No. I thought we were going home?"

Harper snorted. "You can go home and play Nintendo anytime. How often do you get to check out a crime scene with a dead body? *Another* dead body, apparently?"

"Never. I'm not going anywhere near it." Pius was not only afraid of dead bodies, which he figured was one of the most perfectly reasonable fears on his exhaustive list of phobias, but he was also afraid of what kind of trouble he could get into for purposely going to look for them.

"Come on, Pius."

"We don't even know where it is."

"I heard the woman on the radio say the address. It's not far. And I won't even make you ride fast."

Pius had made the mistake of going to his grandmother's funeral and looking at the body in the casket. Her skin looked like sliced turkey meat. It had given him nightmares for weeks, and he still couldn't eat turkey and cheese sandwiches. "No. You can go if you want, I'm going home."

"What if there's a serial killer out there, Pius? What if he's on the loose? You're going to ride home by yourself? Or let me go off by myself?"

"Now that's not fair..." Harper knew Pius was afraid of serial killers. He had heard the case of "Connecticut River Killer" on *Unsolved Mysteries* once and it had freaked him out so bad he couldn't watch television by himself anymore. Not just *Unsolved Mysteries*, any television. He would break out in cold sweat and hives if he was even in a room with a tv set by himself.

And if he even heard the theme song from *Unsolved Mysteries*, he would be reduced to a slobbering mess of tears and urine.

"It's safer if we stick together," said Harper.

"I hate you," said Pius. "Just ride slow, please, I'm getting a charlie horse."

Thirty minutes later, which was about twenty minutes later than Harper thought it should have taken, Pius and Harper arrived on O'Dell Drive. To her credit, Harper only complained once about how long it took – that Pius could hear.

The road was closed off by police cars and barricades, and they were not letting anyone through. Fortunately, Harper knew a short cut, so they rode to the next street over, ditched their bikes, and climbed over a fence. Harper had to give Pius considerable help to get over the head-height wooden barricade, which would have embarrassed some boys, but Pius didn't complain. He would be the first to admit he would never have made it over without his cousin's help. And since it was her stupid idea to come here in the first place, then she should darn right struggle to get his uncoordinated butt over the fence.

The pair crept along the fence, through someone's unmowed backyard, and behind an overgrown bush between two houses, directly across the street from the crime scene. They couldn't make out anything for all the police cars, ambulances and uniformed people milling about.

"Do you know who lives there?" Harper whispered.

"Not a clue. The only person I know who lives on this street is Skidmark."

"What's up, appropriate age-group peers?"

The voice came from behind the pair, catching them both completely off-guard. Pius actually squeaked in alarm.

Harper reared back to punch whoever had crept up on them but stopped at the last second. "Skidma— Brian? What are you doing here?"

"I live here." The small round child pointed at the yellow house behind them. He had a melting, dripping purple popsicle on his hand. "You came to my birthday party in first grade, Pius, remember?"

Pius had no recollection of that, and he could remember pi to forty places.

"What's going on over there?" Harper saved her cousin by pointing across the street.

"Oh, Mrs. Noteworthy died last night." Skidmark sucked on the popsicle. "My dad found her, actually. He always mows her lawn on Saturday morning while I'm watching ProStars. He uses her old electric lawnmower because she doesn't pay him for it so he says he'll be damned if he uses his gas on her lawn. But he keeps running over the extension cord with the mower and he's replaced it at least four times, so it probably would have been cheaper for him to just use gas and his own mower."

"Brian," said Pius. He didn't really want to ask the question but knew if he didn't stop him Skidmark would keep talking for an hour, and before they knew it, he would be telling them about his mom's chronic yeast infections. Again. "Do they know how she died?"

Skidmark took a long suck on his popsicle. It made a gross slurping sound, and when he pulled it away it left a long, violet string of gooey slime hanging between the stick and his lips. "She got hit by lightning."

"WHAT?" Pius and Harper asked in unison.

"Well, they don't actually believe me. I told my dad I saw lightning hit Mrs. Noseworthy's house last night but he doesn't believe me. He thinks I watch too many horror movies and then he asked what I was doing up at two in the morning anyway, so I told him I was watching horror movies, duh. Actually I was watching Star Trek re-runs on CBC but I was just being a jerk to him because he never believes me when I tell him anything. Like that time my little sister was keeping a chipmunk in her bedroom and everyone kept asking where those weird noises were coming from and I told them Lucy had a chipmunk but no, no one ever believes Skidmark..."

"Brian!" Harper said, firmly. "What happened?"

"Well, the chipmunk got into the wall and I guess it got stuck and died because it started to smell..."

"No! Brian, what happened last night? You said you saw lightning?"

"Yeah, I was watching Star Trek and I got up to get some Dunkaroos. It was really stormy outside and there was lightning flashing all over the sky so I stopped to watch it in the dining room window." He pointed back at the Noseworthy house again, a small simple dwelling with beige vinyl siding. "Then I saw this big lightning bolt come out of nowhere right on top of Mrs. Noseworthy's house. I said some bad words my parents told me I'm not allowed to repeat in polite company—I know Pius doesn't count in that but I don't know you very well Harper, so I will spare you the profanity on account of your sensitive feminine ears."

"Jumping murphy, barf-breath, just get on with it! The lightning—was it blue?"

"Yeah, I guess. Cerulean, I guess, technically, maybe sort of aquamarine?"

"Skidma—Brian." Harper took the boy, who was much shorter than her, by the shoulders and looked into his eyes. Pius felt nervous from the intensity of her stare standing two metres away, but Brian was completely nonplussed. He took another lick of his popsicle. "Brian, this is the most important part. Did the lightning bolt come down or up?"

For once, Skidmark said nothing. He actually seemed thoughtful, twisting the purple ice stick in his mouth while looking up at the sky. "You know, now that you mention it. I think it did go up. That's extra weird, isn't it? My dad said it was impossible. He said that if lightning struck her house there would be burn marks somewhere, but apparently he didn't see anything anywhere. The cops asked him a bunch of questions but no one seems to have any idea what happened."

"Except that Mrs. Noseworthy was over eighty years old," Pius said. He could see where Harper was going with this. Making up some sort of *Unsolved Mysteries*-level conspiracy to connect Mrs. Noseworthy's death to whatever they saw over the bay last night was a stretch, to say the least. It would be like Skidmark trying to pull on a pair of Speedos—painful, awkward and just embarrassing all around. "Harper, why don't we just look at the most obvious solution. Occam's Razor. Mrs. Noseworthy probably just had a heart attack or something."

Harper folded her arms and shook her head, her black hair bouncing. "Pius, I don't care about stupid Gillette commercials. Three upside lightning bolts in one night seem awfully strange, doesn't it?"

"Maybe Mrs. Noseworthy took a heart attack climbing in her tree?" Skidmark finished his popsicle and tossed the stick aside. "Ladies her age probably shouldn't exert themselves like that."

"Don't litter like that," Harper scolded. She glared at Skidmark until he picked up the popsicle stick. "What do you mean, climbing her tree?"

"Come see."

Skidmark looked at the popsicle stick in his hands, couldn't decide what to do with it, then shrugged and stuffed it into the pocket of his grey sweatpants. He waved for the others to follow, and led them across his yard, across the street to a house a few doors down from the crime scene.

"Where are we going?" Pius asked. He had a bad feeling about this.

"We can cut around back of the Shelleys' yard to Mrs. Noseworthy's place."

"No!" Pius snapped, louder than he had intended. He looked around to make sure no adults overheard, then lowered his voice. "We're not going to sneak into a crime scene."

"Don't you want to see Mrs. Noseworthy's body?" Skidmark asked.

"No!" Pius exclaimed.

"Yes!" said Harper.

They had both spoken at the same time. They looked at each other, and Harper spoke first. "Okay, fine, you stay here. Give us a holler if the killer comes back, okay?"

Pius looked at the line of cop cars down the street, at the yellow caution tape. He had a horrible, awful feeling in the pit of his stomach, and it wasn't just the slightly out-dated milk he'd put on his cereal, the grueling ride to Keeping and then over here, or finding out his dad was basically illiterate. He was afraid, and for once he didn't think most people would disagree with him. Though he wouldn't admit it to Harper, there was something weird going on. The upside-down lightning. The bodies. Yes, it wasn't just Mrs. Noseworthy. The lady on the radio had said, "We found *another* one." How many dead bodies were piling up today? It didn't make sense.

He wanted nothing more than to go home and hide in his room and play Game Boy, but there was no way he was going anywhere by himself today or any time soon. Nor was he going to wait around only a hundred metres from a possible murder scene, all by himself. Sure, getting closer to the body was hardly better, but at least he wouldn't be alone. And no one said he actually had to *look* at the body. They probably had it covered up by now if it wasn't gone altogether.

"I hate you," Pius breathed.

Harper smiled. "Love you, cuz."

They crept through a backyard full of dog turds, though fortunately, the canine who'd deposited them was nowhere in sight. Skidmark said the Shelleys' had gone to their cabin for the weekend. They climbed another fence—well, Harper and Skidmark climbed the fence. Skidmark was surprisingly limber for a boy with the shape and density of a bowling ball. The two of them had to then awkwardly pull Pius over the fence. He scraped his hands and knees when he landed on the other side.

They pushed through another line of bushes until they found themselves on the edge of Mrs. Noseworthy's property, looking right at the dark blue-pants butt of a police officer standing on the grass right in front of them.

From their vantage point in the bushes, and with the cop's backside blocking their view, the kids couldn't see much. There were a half-dozen police officers in the small yard, including some taking pictures, and there were a couple of medical-looking technicians with a stretcher. There was nothing on the stretcher, though, nor could Pius make out a body anywhere.

Skidmark elbowed the other two kids and pointed up. Pius and Harper followed his chubby finger up, up toward the tallest tree in the yard. There, dangling five metres above their heads, was the body of Mrs. Noseworthy.

She was upside down and completely naked. Pius didn't take his time to look at any fine details; he immediately turned, closed his eyes and tried not to throw up. Unfortunately, he did catch a glimpse of her face, and now he couldn't get that image out of his head. Her eyes were lifeless but wide open, and her mouth was open and her lips pulled back over her teeth like she was in mid-scream. She looked absolutely terrified. Like she had somehow died of terror, and her face froze in the last position it would ever know.

"See?" asked Skidmark. "Isn't that messed up?"

Pius opened his eyes. He heard Skidmark and Harper talking, but he wasn't paying attention to their whispered words. He was looking in the opposite direction, through the trees and bushes where they were hiding. He had only opened his eyes and looked in the first place because he had gotten a horrible feeling that they were being watched.

Red slitted eyes were staring back at Pius through the trees. He locked gazes with it for just a moment, one fleeting moment that seemed to stretch out forever. It was like sitting in the chair waiting for the dentist, only a thousand times worse. He knew that whatever was behind those eyes wanted to kill him, and there would be nothing he could do to stop it.

Pius heard a blood-curdling scream, realizing only after the fact that he was the one who'd made it.

"What in the—" The cop in front of them started to turn. Harper dove into the bushes and dragged Skidmark with her. "Scatter!" she hissed.

Pius found himself on his feet and running before he knew it. He wasn't sure if he was running from the mounties or the eyes he's seen in the trees, all he knew was that he was moving faster than he ever had.

"Stupid kids," the cop muttered.

It took Pius a long time to realize nothing was chasing him. When he finally stopped, he was four streets away. The knee was torn out of his pants and he had scraped up both palms. He was also missing a sneaker.

Pius collapsed where he was, on the lawn of someone he didn't know, gasping for breath and shivering. Harper and Skidmark caught up shortly. Skidmark was breathing nearly as hard as Pius, but Harper just looked angry.

"What're you doing, cracker?" she yelled at him, her voice very nearly a scream.

"I saw... I saw something... In the bushes." Pius could barely get the words out. Between the fear and the lack of oxygen to his brain, he felt like someone was trying to pull his insides out with a grappling hook attached to a snowmobile.

"A dog?" Harper growled. "A seagull? A flipping chipmunk?"

"I saw... glowing red eyes..."

"Pius. I'm sorry because you're my cousin, but you're an idiot and a chicken." Harper threw her hands up in frustration. "There were no glowing red eyes!"

"Actually," said Skidmark. "While both of these things are not exclusive to my observation, I saw them, too."

"What?"

"I saw the eyes. Early this morning, when I snuck over the first time to check out what had happened. They freaked me right out, like portals to the underworld burning plasma beams into my soul. It's like after seeing those eyes I forgot how to love a little bit. I think I genuinely care a little bit less about my sister now."

Harper and Pius stared at Skidmark, stunned. Neither of them knew what to say. Skidmark shrugged. "It's okay. I never really liked her that much to begin with."

"How the heck did she get up into that tree?" Harper shook her head.

"Weird old person gymnastics?" suggested Skidmark, his sister forgotten.

"Butt naked?" asked Harper.

"Old people are into weird stuff," said Skidmark.

"Maybe the force of the lightning bolt?" Harper suggested. "Threw her through the air?"

"I don't think lightning works like that," replied Pius. "And like Brian said, there's no burn marks anywhere."

"Maybe someone cleaned it up while I was blacked out for three hours?" suggested Skidmark. Harper and Pius both whipped around and looked at him. "What? What are you looking at me like that for?"

"You 'blacked out' for three hours?"

"Last night after I saw the lightning bolt. I lost three hours. I thought maybe I fell asleep or something but nope." He whistled and made a whooshing motion with his hand, like a rocket taking off. "Just gone."

Harper's mouth hung open. "Why didn't you tell us about any of this before?"

He shrugged. "I dunno. Guess it didn't seem important."

"You're an idiot. Jumpings, Skidmark, that's it. I'm not calling you Brian anymore. It's just Skidmark."

"That's okay. Even my mom calls me that."

There was a crack of thunder and the sky opened up, unleashing a fresh torrent of rain. The kids ran for cover as regular, old-fashioned lightning leapt across the sky.

## CHAPTER NINE
*Even Better Than The Real Thing*
August 22, 12:40am

On the north edge of town, at the end of a quiet, wooded street off the Harmon Highway, Dick Jeddore stumbled back into his house. It was well past midnight. He had tried to come home several times throughout the day but the weather just kept turning bad. A road washed out in Keeping, stranding half a dozen families, and he volunteered to go help people get evacuated. Some frantic mothers reported a pair of missing teens and Dick worried they would end up dead like the others, but it turned out they just went to make out behind the old dump and were stranded when the road back to town got washed out.

Dick struggled to take off his muddy, damp boots. They had soaked through so many times in the last twenty-four hours he'd lost count. His socks were damp and his feet smelled so bad he nearly gagged. He would have to throw them out; if Harper found them in the laundry, she would have his head. She swore the odour from his stink feet got on everything and wouldn't come out.

The crazy day had kept him so busy he hadn't had much time to think about what was bothering him. About the little tidbit about

Robert Hulan that Cheryl had told him about over the radio that morning.

*"According to the preliminary coroner's report, the victim drowned in saltwater."*

Saltwater. How was that possible? The water supply was kilometres from the bay. So unless someone had dragged the dead man from the beach all the way up to the backside of town...

Gladys from the nursing home had to be lying. The nursing home was just a stone's throw from the ocean, just across the road from the beach. What if Robert Hulan had wandered out and drowned in the ocean... and then what? The home covered it up by dumping his body in the water supply? Why would they do that?

Then there were the Quinn brothers. That's what really complicated the situation. Mike and Will Quinn drowned on the deck of their boat. Three men, dead by drowning in unusual situations, all within hours of each other. That had to be some kind of connection, right?

And then there was Mrs. Noseworthy. He had heard reports of the old woman, found dead outside her house on O'Dell Drive. He hadn't gotten any details and it might have been unrelated, but something about it didn't sit right with him. Four deaths in one day? Either the town was officially cursed, or there was something sinister going on.

He was just tired. Once he got some rest, it would all make sense, or he would realize it was all insane. Either way, sleep would make it better. Unfortunately, as he crossed through his small kitchen, tossing his keys on the table and heading for the brown-carpeted living room, he discovered rest was not meant to be.

Harper was lying asleep on the couch. What the hell was she doing here? She was supposed to be at his brother's place. Why did

Ray let Harper come back here by herself? And why was Pius lying on the floor next to her?

He reached to wake up the kids and decided against it. They must have been up late, and there was no sense disturbing them now. Let them sleep. He considered calling his brother but again, it was almost one a.m. He could wait until tomorrow to yell at him. Normally he would relish the chance to chew out his older brother, but tonight he was just too tired. Dick grabbed some blankets from the closet and was throwing them over the kids when he noticed something clutched in Harper's right hand. It was her pocket knife—a small blade he had given her for her tenth birthday. Why would she go to sleep with a knife in her hand? Carefully, he removed it, folded the blade and laid it on the end table beside her. That's when he noticed a folded piece of paper in her other hand. He took that as well, opened, and read it.

*"Dad—wake me up, I have something important to tell you."*

Weird. She must have been trying to stay up to meet him, but knew she might fall asleep so she left a note. Smart girl. What could be so important that it couldn't wait until tomorrow? Did it have something to do with her going to bed with a knife? Alarm bells started to go off in Dick's head. Once again, he reached to wake his sleeping daughter, but something stopped his hand just before it touched her shoulder.

Movement. The old maroon-coloured velour curtains were mostly drawn over the living-room window, but a small crack remained open and light from a street lamp shined through. Something moved across the yard, momentarily blocking the light.

Though the rain had stopped, it was still quite windy outside. Blowing branches could have caused the weird moving shadows that caught Dick's attention.

Except there were no trees on that side of the house.

Dick Jeddore moved quietly to the window and peered through the curtains. The yard was clear, the world was wet, and the grass looked grey in the dim light. But there was nothing out there but his truck, parked in the gravel driveway.

There was a knock at the door.

Dick nearly jumped out of his skin.

Who could be at his door at this hour? A million thoughts rushed through his mind, none of them good. One of them was to grab a weapon, but there was nothing within easy reach. His guns were locked up in the basement, his hunting knives were upstairs or in the truck. Even the sports and camping supplies were in the shed.

The front door was off the kitchen, and through the darkened living room he could see all the way to the grey, metal door. There was a small window in it, covered by a thin gauzy curtain that his sister-in-law had put up, telling him he needed more privacy, especially with a young girl in the house. Through the curtain, he could make out the indistinct shape of someone standing outside the door, and suddenly Dick felt cold all over. The hair on his neck stood up, and the air felt thick with static electricity.

Two red eyes glowed from the figure at the door.

Despite the cold, Dick broke out into a sweat. Strong fingers squeezed his heart, and he wanted to run. Out the back door, to his truck, and get as far away from here as possible. In a heartbeat, all his grandmother's old stories came back to haunt him. *Malsum. Lox. Wendigo.* He was pretty sure she had just read the words in a book somewhere and made the rest up, but it still terrified him as a kid.

He couldn't run. Not with Harper and Pius lying on the floor. He had to protect his family and would do anything to keep them safe, even if that meant confronting whatever was outside that door.

Dick moved slowly to the kitchen, his sock feet making not a sound. He could creep up on a moose through dry autumn brush; sneaking through his own kitchen without boots on was a piece of cake. Still, it was the hardest and most difficult thing he had ever done. If he spooked a moose, it would just run away and he might have to spend a few hours tracking it down again. If he spooked whatever was outside that door... For some reason Dick doubted it would run away.

There were knives in the drawer by the sink. They weren't his field knife or a hunting rifle, but they would have to do. He could gut a salmon with his eyes closed, surely he could take care of whatever was out there...

He thought of the dead old man. Of the two guys in the boat, of the old lady that he hadn't actually seen, but had heard the report over the radio. It was too much of a coincidence that they all dropped dead within a few hours of each other. He couldn't imagine what had killed them, but could this... whatever it was, have something to do with it? And what was it doing here, at his house?

Dick reached for the knife drawer. Slowly, slowly, his eyes never leaving the window. The glowing red dots in the window never blinked, but the form did move slightly, as if breathing hard or swaying in the wind. He was sure the eyes could see what he was doing. What would it do when he pulled out a knife? How fast could it...

The phone rang and Dick nearly crapped his pants. It was piercing in the quiet still night air. He glanced at the kids, who hadn't moved, and then back at the door.

The eyes, and the shadow, were gone.

The phone rang again, and Dick finally took a breath. He had no idea how long he had been holding it. The kids hadn't stirred yet, but that wouldn't last if it kept ringing. He wasn't ready to talk with them yet.

Dick crossed the kitchen and grabbed the phone off the wall before it rang a third time.

## INTERMÈDE

*It felt hungry, possibly hungrier than before.*

*Worse, it was strong enough now to know it was in danger. Someone knew it was. They may not know how or why, but it knew that it was, and that was far too much.*

*It had been on the way back home when it felt the danger. The one who knew. It veered off course to investigate. Was it strong enough yet, to deal with someone who knew what it was? Who might be able to fight back? So far it had fed upon weak prey, or taken them by surprise. This body was so frail, it could not stand up to direct conflict with a motivated opponent.*

*At least, not yet.*

*If it could kill the Hunter, it would speed up the regeneration process considerably. Old people, while easy to kill, had so little life force it was barely worth it. Even those men on the boat were weak of mind, their souls gave little more nourishment than a warm glass of watered-down ale.*

*But this Hunter; he was strong. Willful. Tasty. He would go a long way to building enough power to shed this pathetic mortal shell and reclaim its true shape. And he was tired now, distracted. Ripe for the picking. There would be no better time.*

*It approached the Hunter's dwelling, could sense it inside; could sense other young, vital life sources. Perhaps it could regain all the power it needed right now, in one single strike. It just needed to act quickly, while the element of surprise was on its side...*

*The Hunter sensed its presence. It could feel the change in his mind, his heightened awareness. He was expecting it now, even if he did not know what it was. That was unfortunate, but not insurmountable. It would just have to move quickly before the others awoke...*

*What was that indomitable noise?*

## CHAPTER TEN

*Knocking On Heaven's Door*

August 22, 12:55am

Niall had spent most of the day at the nursing home. After the incident with Nana, his parents had a lot of questions for the staff. He thought for a while that they may be bringing her back home with them, but ultimately they left Nana with the supposedly competent employees of the Western Health Nursing Home.

He never told his parents about what he heard from Mr. Jeddore. His mom was already upset, he didn't want to make it worse. Plus he wasn't supposed to have heard what Mr. Jeddore and the nurse were talking about, and that nurse wasn't supposed to tell Mr. Jeddore, either. Niall was afraid that if he started spreading that news, both himself and others would get in trouble.

Besides, it was probably just a fluke with that old guy, right? Old people passed away in places like this all the time. That was why they sent old people to nursing homes. They should call them death centres, instead of homes, really. It was only an unfortunate accident that Mr. Hulan had died the way he did. There was no way that could happen twice, right?

The wind and rain picked up on their drive home, going over Micmac Head. Niall's mom experienced a brief panic attack, and Niall himself admitted he was pretty freaked out for those few moments the rain was coming down so hard he couldn't see through the windshield.

Still, his dad handled it all well. His boring, still demeanour served him well by keeping him calm and cool as a dead fish in stressful situations. It wasn't so good when Niall had something important to talk about, but it got them home in one piece. The rain never let up, though. Niall asked if he could go over to Pius' now, but his mom said there was no way he or anyone else was going back out in that storm. Niall tried to call but there was no answer.

Niall went to bed early and spent a long time staring at the ceiling. He also spent a fair bit of time staring at his poster of Michelle Pfeiffer. That didn't interest him as much as usual, his thoughts continually drifting back to Harper. And his grandmother. And dead old people. It really killed the fantasies he usually had while lying in bed, that's for sure.

He picked up his Game Boy and played Tetris for a while, but he was barely interested in that as well. When the battery light came on, he tossed it aside without a second thought. He tried picking up a Youngblood comic but couldn't concentrate on it. Joey Smallwood came into his room and crawled over the Ninja Turtles blankets at the foot of his bed for a while. The fluffy yellow cat howled at Niall for not being Nana, allowed the boy to scratch him once behind the ears, then hissed at him and wandered away. Joey Smallwood made Niall think about Nana again, which made it even more difficult to read about scantily-clad women with giant boobs and muscle-bound thugs with no necks or feet.

Finally Niall gave up, turned off the light and rolled over. He listened to the wind and the rain outside until it lulled him off to sleep.

He dreamed of his Nana. At least he thought it was her. It was a much younger woman, not much older than him. She looked a bit like his mom. She kinda looked like Harper too, actually, which freaked him out a bit when he put his mom and his crush side-by-side.

The woman was standing at the edge of a cliff overlooking the ocean. The sky was dark, and a strong wind whipped at her black hair and long, old-fashioned dress. Niall felt cold, which was weird. He never remembered feeling cold in a dream before.

The woman turned toward him. She had a slight smile on her face, which really reminded him of his mother, but it faded quickly. Her humour turned to fear and horror. She stared at Niall, stared through him, until he began to think that he was the one that was causing her fear. Then he realized she was looking at someone *behind* him, and tried to turn around. He couldn't. His feet were rooted to the ground like trees grown deep in the earth.

She opened her mouth but nothing came out. Still, Niall could make out the words perfectly from the shape of her lips.

"Help me," she screamed without a sound.

And then the woman was falling, disappeared over the edge of the cliff. Niall could move again, and he chased after her, but by the time he reached the edge, she was long gone. There was nothing below him but rocks and crashing waves.

Niall awoke shivering. He heard his parents talking in the kitchen.

"It's okay, it will be okay," he heard his father say. Niall felt his forehead. Why was he so wet? He must have been sweating something awful.

"How?" his mother was saying. "How will she be okay out in the storm like this? Why won't the police do anything?"

Niall looked at the clock. One AM. what were his parents doing up? Were they watching a movie or something?

A thought struck Niall and he felt his stomach tighten. He threw up a little in his mouth and choked it back down. He was disgusted by the taste of things he didn't remember eating.

Though he dreaded the answer, he had to know. Dressed in his damp, under-sized pyjamas with the detective in the yellow-fedora on the front, he crawled out of bed and staggered down the hall toward the kitchen.

"How could this happen?" His mom's voice. "How could they let her just walk away?"

He didn't hear his dad's answer, because they heard him approaching and his dad called out, "Niall, what are you doing up?"

"I heard you talking." It wasn't a lie. He came around the corner and saw his parents sitting at the table. They were in their pyjamas as well, though theirs fit and neither of them had a 1930s detective or gangster in sight.

"I'm sorry, Niall," his mom said. She was clutching the phone in her hands and her eyes were red. She had been crying. "Go back to bed."

She grabbed Niall in a fierce hug and squeezed him. He knew there was something wrong. He could just tell, she didn't even need to say anything. And he knew what it was. Still he had to ask.

"Mom, is everything okay?"

"Everything is fine," she said into Niall's hair, and he could feel her shaking. "Please go back to bed."

"Okay. Tell me in the morning, okay."

"I will. I love you."

"Love you, too, mom."

Niall broke the hug and walked back down the hall, but he didn't go into his room. He walked down to the end, to his parents' room. They had another phone in there.

Nana wasn't dead. His mom would have told him if she was dead. Somehow, Niall felt he would have known if she was dead. The woman in his dream asked for help. She couldn't ask for help if she was dead.

Niall quietly closed his parents' door, sat down on their unmade bed, and picked up the phone receiver. The grey, spiral cord swayed freely against his arm a moment as he stared at the buttons. He was pretty sure he remembered the number. He didn't want to wake up the wrong person in the middle of the night.

Niall sighed and dialled the number. He realized his pyjamas were so damp he was getting his parents' blankets wet. The phone rang on the other end of the line.

A thought suddenly occurred to him. Had he wet himself? Is that why he was so wet? He jumped up, the phone still ringing. No, he was drenched from head to foot. There was no way he could have peed that much.

A familiar voice said "Hello?" on the other end of the line.

Niall smelled the sleeve of his pyjamas. Then he tasted it and scrunched up his face. Salt water? How—?

"Hello?" the voice asked again.

Niall snapped out of it and turned his attention back to the phone.

"Hello, Mister Jeddore?" said Niall. "I need your help."

# CHAPTER ELEVEN

*Jump Around*

August 22, 1:35am

Dick hung up the receiver on the wall, then turned and glared at Niall. "I told your parents you're here. Needless to say, they were surprised, but I told them you were upset about your grandmother and you wanted to see your friends."

Niall was sitting on the couch between Harper and Pius. He was soaking wet and wrapped in a blanket, on account of riding his bike over here in a rainstorm.

"Thank you," Niall said, his hands shaking on a cup of hot chocolate.

"I told you we could talk about this in the morning."

"And I told you it couldn't wait." Niall stared at him, his blue eyes burning into him. "You know why."

The kid was right. He wanted to tell him not to worry, that the RCMP would find his grandmother, but he knew it was a lie. He had actually called the detachment after he got off the phone with Niall the first time, and the constable on duty told him they had no resources or intention to send anyone out in the storm to look for a senile old woman. Dick reminded the guy that four other people had died the night before, but even that did nothing to move him. The constable must have had strict orders from Sergeant Tanguay.

"So let's go over this again. What exactly did you guys see last night?"

The kids told him again. About the blue lightning, travelling from the ground up, right in the middle of the bay where the Quinn brothers had died. And the story from the Brian Hawco kid, who claimed he had seen the exact same lightning right where they found Mrs. Noseworthy hanging dead and naked from a tree. It was all so strange, like a bad science fiction story, but the cases were too weird to be just coincidences. He had always suspected the deaths were connected. He just couldn't imagine there was some magical, Freddy Krueger villain behind it.

Then Pius told him about what he saw at Noseworthy's place. "What exactly did you see?" he asked his nephew again.

Pius was shaken. "Just eyes. Glowing red eyes, like burning embers. It was more of a feeling. I felt cold and empty like I was somewhere very far away. Like I was all dead inside."

"He was staring at it for a long time, Dad," added Harper. "He was just looking off into the bushes for like five minutes before he started screaming."

"Five minutes?" asked Pius. "No way. It couldn't have been more than a few seconds."

"Seriously, Pius. Skidmark and I watched one of the cops eat a whole box of Timbits, and you didn't move a muscle the entire time."

Crap. The time distortion fit with what he himself had felt. He thought he had been staring at the eyes in the window for only a moment, but when he looked at the clock he realized he'd lost nearly half-an-hour. And the kids had described losing even more time when they saw the lightning. "Dad, what's wrong?" asked Harper.

"I saw it too. It was here just earlier tonight."

The kids looked at each other in horror and shock. Maybe he shouldn't have told them that. He was the adult here, they all looked to him for reassurance and explanation. But he had neither, and he was too tired to fake it. "Look, there's something weird going on here. I don't know what, but I'm going to the Crossing to look for Niall's grandmother."

"What about us?" asked Pius.

Dick grabbed his keys and headed for the door. "You are staying here."

Pius looked like Dick had kicked his puppy.

"Dad," called Harper. "You're going to leave us here? With the psycho hose beast you just saw outside?"

Shoot. Okay maybe that wasn't such a good idea. "Go. Get in the truck. Harper, grab some flashlights from the cupboard by the fridge." He turned and headed downstairs.

"Where are you going?" his daughter asked.

"Go get in the truck!" Dick called back without stopping or turning around. At the bottom of the creaky wooden stairs, he flicked on the lights for the small, dirt-walled, cellar-like room. As he walked past the water heater and fuse box, he pulled the keys for the gun cabinet out of his pants pocket.

# CHAPTER TWELVE

*Thunder Kiss '65*

August 22, 2:10am

"Are you sure you can see where you're going, Uncle Dick?" asked Pius for the fourth time. Even Niall could tell the forestry officer was getting annoyed by his nephew's constant questions, but Pius was not good at reading a room.

"Pius, I need to concentrate on the road." Mr. Jeddore's hands were gripped on the steering wheel, his knuckles white. "Now is not the time."

The windshield of the truck was a blurry mess of pounding rain. The front seat was crammed with all four of them in the cab, but Mr. Jeddore's truck didn't have a back seat. Harper was closest to her dad, buckled into the same belt as Pius. Niall wished he could have been the one to share a seatbelt with Harper, but he couldn't come up with a way to suggest it without sounding weird.

They had driven out of town, through the airfield of old hangars the locals called "The Ramp," but the rain was so heavy and it was so dark they didn't even see any of it. Mr. Jeddore kept the low beams on because whenever he turned on the highs, they could see nothing but an opaque wall of swirling rain, but that, unfortunately, meant all they could see was less than a dozen metres of the road directly in front of them. They didn't even see the match stick factory when they drove past it, and only realized they had reached Micmac Head when the road suddenly started to rise steeply upward. Driving over the Head, slower than Niall had ever seen anyone drive, was still faster than he would have liked. Not that he would say anything. He wouldn't let anyone—especially Harper—know he was scared out of his freaking mind. Not that it mattered. Pius was expressing more than enough fear and apprehension for both of them.

"I think you're going too fast, Uncle Dick." Pius' hand was gripping Niall's arm even tighter than Mr. Jeddore was gripping the steering wheel. Niall really wished they had left him home, and not just because it would let him sit closer to Harper.

"Shut up, Pius," said Mr. Jeddore.

"I just think, based on the reduced friction of the asphalt and the low visibility, your reaction time and stopping distance are going to be way longer than..."

"Shut up, Pius!" snapped Harper.

Niall's eyes were glued to the road. He could see the bare rock cliff on the right, and they were coming up on the turn with the steep drop-off on their left. They were almost over the worst of it, then it would just be a long hill down the other side. Which would also be problematic, but one thing at a time.

Even with all of his attention focused on the road and the wipers going at full speed, Niall still didn't see the woman until they were upon her. Mr. Jeddore saw her a half-a-second after him, and by then it was too late. Niall started to scream "watch out!" but the truck was already swerving to avoid her. Then the world was blocked out by screams—both his and Harper's and especially Pius'. The truck spun out. He couldn't see anything through the blurry windshield, but they all felt it when they hit the barricade on the left side of the road and suddenly the truck was flipping over and Pius couldn't tell which way was up or which way was down.

The last thing Niall remembered was the eyes. The woman standing in the road had glowing red eyes.

Niall wasn't sure how long it was before he woke up, but when he did, he was definitely upside down. He was still in the cab of the truck, and the truck was upside down on the side of the embankment. His seatbelt was all that was keeping him strapped to the seat.

"Harper?" He heard Mr. Jeddore's voice. "Kids? Harper? Are you okay?"

His voice sounded panicked. He was really worried. Niall tried to speak but no words came out. It took him a moment to swim out of the fuzziness in his head and back into the real world. He reached out in the darkness and haze and his fingers touched something warm and sticky. Was it... blood?  He suddenly felt more awake. "Mister Jeddore... I'm here..."

"Niall! Niall don't move!" He heard a glimmer of hope in Mr. Jeddore's voice, but the terror was still there. "We're upside down, and the truck is teetering on the edge of the bank. We're okay!"

Niall wanted to give him the benefit of the doubt, seeing how Mr. Jeddore was the adult in the situation, but what he really wanted to ask was "How in the hell are we okay?"

"How's Harper and Pius?" Niall asked instead.

"They're unconscious but breathing." It was very dark in the cab of the truck, none of the lights were on, and the windows were obscured by water and mud. He could hear the rain pounding on the undercarriage. He heard Mr. Jeddore fumbling with the radio and cursed under his breath. "The radio's dead. Look, I'm going to try and crawl out, and then pull you kids out behind me, okay?"

Niall nodded. He wasn't sure if Mr. Jeddore could see him, but he heard the grunt and shuffle as the man arranged himself. The door opened, just a little, and Mr. Jeddore grunted to shove it wide enough for him to fit through.

As soon as Mr. Jeddore started to slide out, Niall knew something was wrong. He felt the truck shifting beneath his head. He heard the creak of metal, the crumbled growling of rocks and dirt letting go.

"Mr. Jeddore!" Niall hissed through gritted teeth. He tried not to think about how far it was down to the ground below. He had no idea how long it was. Ten meters? Fifty? It looked so far from the road above... "The truck is moving..."

"I know, I know." The panic was palpable in the man's voice now. In the dim light, Niall could see he was mostly out of the truck now, with just his head and one arm inside the door. "We have to move fast. Can you reach up and unbuckle Pius and Harper's seat belt? I'll pull them toward me and that should balance the weight..."

The creaking grew louder and Niall's stomach lurched. He didn't even get a chance to look for the buckle. The truck started to slide and suddenly Mr. Jeddore was gone, and the driver's door slammed shut with a weird thud. It must have hit him in the head.

For the second time in minutes, Niall felt weightless. This time the feeling seemed to last for a very long time.

## CHAPTER THIRTEEN

*Crucify*

August 22, 1:00pm

Dick crawled up from the bottom of a very dark, cold pool of water. He immediately wished he hadn't.

Everything hurt. His body ached, his stomach churned, his head was spinning and he hadn't even opened his eyes. Hell, even his eyelids hurt. How did his eyelids hurt?

What happened? Where was he? Where was…

Harper?

"Where's Harper?" Dick Jeddore asked, trying to sit up and immediately driven back down onto the bed by the pain. He was in a hospital. Oh, God, the truck had gone over the cliff on Micmac Head, and now he was in the hospital. "Where are the kids?" he groaned. His throat was dry and scratchy. Something was in his nose and wires and hoses were attached to his chest and arms.

Sergeant Tanguay was there, for some reason, sitting in the only chair in the room. She was dressed in her uniform of grey shirt and dark blue pants. Her cap was sitting on the side table beside his bed. "Don't move," she said. "The doctors said you probably have a concussion."

"Where are the kids?" Jeddore asked again. "Where's Harper?"

There was a long pause before the Sergeant finally answered. "We don't know."

"What do you mean you don't know? Where's my daughter?"

"We found your truck at the bottom of the bank, near Mine Pond. The kids were gone. They must have wandered off."

They were alive then. Thank God. He hadn't killed them. "They couldn't have gone far. Harper would know to head for the road."

"We've looked everywhere, no one has seen them yet. But don't worry, we'll find them."

"Everywhere? There's nowhere they can go down there. How long was I out?"

"About twelve hours."

Twelve hours? He realized now that the blinds of his room were drawn, and he could see the afternoon sun peeking in from the edges. "I've got to go help look for them." Dick again tried to get up, but he couldn't. Everything hurt. Something had to be broken. Maybe every bone in his body.

"You're not going anywhere," said Tanguay. She put a hand on his chest, and even a gentle push left him completely immobile. "The doctor needs to check you for a concussion and a dozen other problems. Plus I have some questions."

It took Jeddore a minute to understand what she was getting at. Then he noticed the notebook in her hands.

"What are you talking about?"

"What the hell were you doing out there in the middle of the night with three kids?"

"It was my daughter and my nephew. And the Niall kid, he showed up at my door at 2 am and I called his parents as soon as he did. Everyone knew they were with me."

Tanguay shook her head. "I'm not trying to insinuate something inappropriate, I just need to know where the hell you were going at three in the morning in the middle of a storm. I have two sets of parents out there that are going to chew you out when they get in here, so you need to help me understand what you were doing so I can try and keep them from killing you."

Jeddore stared at her, speechless. It must have been the drugs because he didn't understand a word she was saying. She sounded like she wanted to help him? He sighed. "Niall was scared because he heard that his grandmother had disappeared from the home. He called me because he saw me at the home yesterday, asking about Robert Hulan."

"And you went to look for her yourself in the middle of the night?"

"Yeah, maybe. I don't know." He closed his eyes. It was so hard to think clearly. "There's just been some weird stuff going on. I wanted to check for myself."

Sergeant Tanguay made a very deliberate show of closing her notebook and slipping it into the pocket of her dress shirt. Her uniform was perfectly pressed, of which Dick was not surprised. She also wore her official necktie, which he had never seen another local officer wear, not even the COs. "What drove you off the road?"

"You won't believe me."

"Try me."

Dick stared at her intense, dark eyes for a long moment. He wasn't even sure she blinked. What did she know? Was she trying to trick him into saying something crazy? To hell with it, if he was crazy, might as well find out for sure.

"There was a woman on the road. I have no idea where she came from. She just materialized out of thin air, and then disappeared again just as quick."

There was a long pause. Finally, Tanguay asked, "Did she have red eyes?"

Jeddore sat bolt upright. Or more specifically, he sat up at about a 45-degree angle, which was the best he could manage. "How did you know?"

"We need to talk," said Sergeant Tanguay.

## CHAPTER FOURTEEN

*Whoomp! (There It Is)*

August 22, 9:00pm

Brian "Skidmark" Hawco looked through the shelves of Jerry's video rental store one last time, making sure he got the right stuff. Jerry, a balding, overweight man in glasses wearing a Grateful Dead t-shirt, was standing at the cash register, looking annoyed.

"It's nine o'clock, kid, I'm closing up." Jerry had a deep, strong voice that would have been perfect for the radio. He tapped a pencil on the side of the register and gestured for Skidmark to bring his rentals to the front.

"Almost done," Skidmark said, thoughtfully. He picked up a movie case from the shelf. "Is *Nightmare on Elm Street Part 4* as good as part 3? I really liked part 3, I thought it took the series in new and interesting directions. I would hate to think it was a backward step, like Friday the 13th part 6 was."

"I don't care, kid, they're all just dumb slasher flicks. Just pick one and get out."

"You have terrible customer service skills, you know that?" said Skidmark, replacing the video on the shelf and taking down another. "Are you trying to alienate a regular paying customer?"

"Yes, actually, that's exactly what I'm trying to do. Is it working?"

"Nope," said Skidmark, replacing the video and picking up another.

He continued to scan the shelves as Jerry banged around behind the counter, noisily putting things away and closing up shop. The radio next to the cash register played the closing chorus to Tom Cochrane's "Life is a Highway," then cut to a short news update about Dick Jeddore and the missing kids, Niall, Pius and Harper. Apparently, there was still no sign of the kids, and Harper's dad was in the hospital in serious condition. The cops had actually come by Skidmark's place earlier that day to ask him questions since, apparently, he had been the last person to talk to Harper and Pius the day before. He explained that the kids had probably been taken by the weird red-eyed monster that had been creeping around Mrs. Noseworthy's house, but the cops had laughed at him. All except that French lady with the scowling face who kinda looked like Deanna Troy from Star Trek. She wasn't nice about it, but at least she didn't laugh, and she asked him a few follow-up questions that made it seem like she was actually taking him seriously.

Finally, at 9:05, Skidmark placed three movies, a 2L bottle of Pepsi, a bag of Hostess chips and a package of Twizzlers on the counter. "Do your parents actually let you watch this stuff?" Jerry asked as he grabbed the tapes from the shelf behind the counter, replacing the black plastic cases with the empty boxes from the shelves that Skidmark had handed him.

"I dunno, do your parents let you watch that stuff?" Skidmark pointed at a plastic shopping bag of videos sitting next to the register. Most of the video names were obscured, but Skidmark could just make out something about "Oily Co-Eds" and another about "Butt"-something.

Jerry snatched the bag and shoved them under the counter. "I am a grown man, and I watch what I want to watch, okay?"

"But you do live with your mom, right?"

"She's old, I take care of her."

Skidmark nodded. "Does she watch the Butt movie with you? That's nice. It must be hard for an older lady to get any action, so even seeing it on TV is probably exciting for her."

"You little pervert." Jerry threw the tapes on the counter. "Get the hell out of my store."

"I didn't pay," said Skidmark, half-heartedly holding out a ten-dollar bill.

"I already closed the register and I don't want to look at you anymore." Jerry shoved Skidmark toward the door so hard the kid nearly fell down the three steps from the store floor to the street level.

"That's very kind of you," said Skidmark as he was bum-rushed out the door. "I really do appreciate your generosity. You know, it's a shame more business owners don't respect their youth clientele and cater to them like you do, knowing that they are in fact the customers of the future who will keep them in business for years to come."

The door slammed closed and locked behind him. He had been inside for nearly two hours, and it was now growing dark. Skidmark smiled and shoved his ten dollar bill back in the pocket of his ill-fitting Adidas shorts, then turned and started to walk West along Main Street, swinging his bag of goodies as he went.

He barely got six steps before nearly running into Keith Doucette.

The much taller boy was dressed in an official Toronto Blue Jays jersey, a backwards MuchMusic cap, and ironically the exact same running shorts Skidmark was wearing. There weren't many places to buy clothes in Gale Harbour.

Keith, instinctively, shoved Skidmark to the ground. "Watch where you're going, Skidmark," he growled, unable to stop his behaviour any more than he could choose to stop breathing. Some teenage girls stepped around the scene and kept walking, whispering amongst themselves.

Skidmark lay on the cool sidewalk, doing nothing, as Keith stepped over him and dragged the toe of his Reebok Pump across his ribs. Skidmark had long ago learned not to retaliate against people like Keith; if you just ignored them and took a small amount of abuse, like name-calling and body-checks into lockers, they usually got bored and moved on before unleashing more serious abuses like assault with an orange in a gym sock, or stuffing raw meat in your pants and shoving you into a caged pen with a feral German Shepherd.

Keith tried the door to Jerry's Video Shack, found it locked, and let fly with a string of swear words usually reserved for a sailor getting his hand caught in a bandsaw. He looked down at Skidmark, still lying on the concrete and staring at the darkening evening sky. "What are you looking at, you retard?"

"The clouds are pretty," said Skidmark. "That one looks like a VF-1A Veritech."

"Stupid weirdo nerd," muttered Keith. He noticed the plastic bag at Skidmark's side. "What's in the bag, Skidmark?"

"Just weirdo nerd stuff," replied Skidmark.

Keith snatched the bag away so hard it nearly took Skidmark's fingers with it. "What's this? *Nightmare on Elm Street*? *Friday the 13th*? You got surprisingly good taste in movies. I can actually watch these myself."

"They've got to go back tomorrow," said Skidmark. "Please don't keep my videos past their due date. Jerry will make me pay a fine!"

"Oooh, not Jerry, oh I'm so afraid of Jerry." Keith waved his hands in mock horror. "Oh, and chips! Thanks for remembering."

"Please man, don't take the tapes. If they don't go back it costs a ton of money." Skidmark learned about that first hand when his little sister tried to flush a rental copy of *Willow* down the toilet after the Eborsisk freaked her out.

"Oh, please bring them back!'" mocked Keith in a high-pitched voice, which in Skidmark's opinion sounded nothing like him. "You're such a little bitch. Piss off."

Keith turned and started to walk away. Skidmark watched him, still lying on the ground. It wasn't even that he might have to pay a fine, or that Keith might beat him up. The problem was that if the tapes didn't come back, Jerry might call his parents and then they would find out what kind of movies he was watching and put a stop to it.

Keith cut down behind the Video Shack, heading behind the 99 Main Street club next door. Even though it was Sunday night, there were still a number of people gathered outside, and cigarette smoke drifted through the open doors. Skidmark finally rolled to his feet, and hoping he would live to regret his decision, he followed Keith.

Skidmark found Keith at the back door to the Brown Bowler, yet another club two doors down from the 99 (Gale Harbour had a shocking number of clubs and bars, per capita), and the younger boy ducked by the side of a dumpster to stay out of sight. Keith waited around for a few minutes until the door opened and a man came out carrying stacked cases of empty beer bottles.

"Is Les working tonight?" Keith asked the man as he put the beer bottles down by the door.

"Nah, he's off Sundays and Mondays."

"Hey, cool, look, you think I can buy a couple of Black Horse off you?"

Black Horse was a cheap beer brewed in Newfoundland, something that Keith was definitely too young to be buying. Skidmark didn't know who Les was, but he imagined he could get in a lot of trouble for selling beer to a kid. This man who was not Les—a middle-aged guy dressed in a tight t-shirt with arms like tree trunks—looked down his nose at Keith. "What are you, kid? Twelve?"

"I'm fourteen," said Keith, managing a surprising amount of cockiness for someone who was being scolded like a little kid.

T-shirt guy rolled his eyes. "Screw off, kid, go play Nintendo." He went back into the club and the door slammed shut.

Keith, dejected, began to poke through the empty bottles the guy had dropped off, apparently looking for some that contained a few dregs. Skidmark considered trying to make a grab for the movies, but Keith never put the bag down. Even if he got them, Skidmark would never be able to outrun the bigger, older boy. Skidmark had famously been the first and only kid at St Paul's Elementary School who had taken over fifteen minutes to finish a 50-metre dash, mostly because he had tripped and hurt himself at the starting line. It worked out, though. If he hadn't had a rest while the gym teacher checked on his ankle, he never would have been able to make the finish line. There would have surely been a great nickname to commemorate that occasion, if "Skidmark" hadn't already been so popular.

Skidmark's parents were terribly disappointed their eldest child had the physical and academic aptitude of a milk crate full of sweaty gym socks (their words), so he really didn't want to add their ire at his choice of movies to their reasons to think less of him. He had to get those movies back, even if it meant crossing Keith to do so.

Realizing his foe was at his weakest, and greatly over-estimating the size of his own balls, Skidmark stepped out from behind the dumpster.

"What the hell do you want, Skidmark?" asked Keith, straightening up so fast he dropped a bottle. It smashed on the ground.

"I want my movies back," said Skidmark.

Keith stared at him in disbelief. "Are you serious? You going to make me give them to you?"

"No, but if you don't give them to me, I'm going to tell everyone at school you're a disgusting alcoholic who drinks from garbage bottles behind the club like a hobo."

That was it. His big Hail Mary shot. He couldn't stand up to Keith physically, socially, and even brains was a toss-up. His only hope was blackmail.

"I'm going to kill you," growled Keith.

Oh well, thought Skidmark. It was worth a try.

Keith took two steps forward and froze. He had spotted something behind Skidmark that gave him pause. The bully stepped back and Skidmark risked a glance over his shoulder to see what had scared the one who usually did the scaring.

There was a tall, old woman by the corner of the building. She was silhouetted by light from a street lamp, her face obscured by shadow. She was dressed in a tracksuit, with a baseball cap pulled down over her eyes.

She stared at them for what seemed like a very long time, roughly the same amount of time that it took Skidmark's mom to check his head for lice every week. He had only had lice once, when he was five, but it grossed his mom out so much that she had continued to check his scalp every Saturday night ever since. Skidmark considered making a break for it, but once again, 15-minute 50-metre dash and all that.

Finally Keith broke the silence. "What are you staring at?"

"Dead boys," said the old woman. Her voice was flat and without emotion.

Keith sniggered. "Yeah, whatever. Look, I'm about to beat the crap out of this retard, so just beat it, okay lady?"

"You should respect your elders," said the old woman. She had a strange accent Skidmark didn't recognize. Was it French? Russian? He was so busy thinking about it that he didn't notice that the woman was suddenly gone, but Keith sure noticed.

"Where the hell did she go?" Keith said, looking around frantically. "She was there and then she just vanished into thin air…"

Skidmark saw the glint of metal below Keith's throat. The bully must have felt it, because he froze. "She's behind me, isn't she?" he whispered.

The glint came from the long blade of a knife held by a frail, wrinkled hand. The old woman looked over Keith's shoulder, her yellow eyes and teeth smiling.

"Yep," said Skidmark.

Instinctively, Keith tried to pull away, and the knife flashed quickly in the dark. Keith screamed and Skidmark saw something flop to the ground at his feet.

"You cut off my ear!" Keith howled. "Why did you do that?"

"You moved."

Keith tried to pull away, but the old lady grabbed him by the other ear and he froze. He held his hands to the side of his head, blood seeping through his fingers.

"You could have warned me!"

Without letting go of the ear that was still attached to his head, the old woman waved the knife in his face with her other hand. "I don't make threats. Now you know not to move unless I tell you. And stop whining, it was only the lobe."

Keith pulled his hand away from his face. The blood looked almost black in the fading light, and he turned deathly pale, like Michael Jackson. "I'm going to die..."

"Stop being such a little bitch," said the old woman, echoing the words Keith had said to Skidmark a few minutes before. Had she been following them? "You'll live."

"You cut off my ear!"

She twisted his good ear. "Do you want me to cut off the other one?"

Keith fell quiet almost instantly. He whimpered and sobbed softly.

"What about you?" asked the old woman, pointing the blade at Skidmark.

"Me? I already peed in my pants several times tonight."

The old woman shook her head. "What? Never mind. Just come with me. Oh, and are either of you claustrophobic?"

## CHAPTER FIFTEEN
*Digging In The Dirt*
August 22, 9:40pm

Marie-Ann Tanguay stepped out of her cruiser on the wooded dirt road behind Mine Pond. Another police car was parked a few meters away, beside a line of yellow police tape that blocked the road entirely. Constable Bennett was standing beside the car, smoking a cigarette that he quickly crushed out.

"Sergeant Tanguay," said Bennett, a little disconcerted. "What brings you out here this wet, dreary August evening?"

"I've just been thinking a lot about this case, and I wanted to have another look around." It wasn't a lie. She had been thinking an awful lot about this—the whole town was, with three kids missing out here somewhere—and she did want to have a look around. "Anything to report?"

"Nothing Sergeant," said Bennett, scratching the back of his head. "We've had people combing the area all day but no one's seen a trace or sign of the kids. Now that it's getting dark most of the volunteers are heading in. I think the last couple just left a few minutes ago."

She nodded, though she already knew all of this, having gotten a briefing from dispatch just moments ago. What she wanted to get was a sense of Bennett's state of mind, and she could tell he was tired and jumpy. He had been here all day and most of last night, so it was hardly surprising. "What time is your shift over?"

"Cooper's relieving me in another hour, he's pulling the night shift."

"Look, I'm going to be around here for awhile, why don't you head out early? You've been out here since last night, haven't you?"

"Yeah," replied Bennett, his thoughts a long way away. "I would love to get home and give my kids a hug, you know what I mean?"

She knew very well what he meant, but she tried not to let her emotions show. Instead, she put on what she hoped was a knowing smile. "Of course, Constable. Get out of here. I'll hold down the fort."

"Thanks, sergeant. I'll be here all the earlier tomorrow." Bennett, not waiting even a second least she changed her mind, hopped into his cruiser and started backing out down the narrow dirt road. Branches actually scraped at the side of his car, which caused Tanguay to flinch. She was sure Bennett wasn't going to fill out the paperwork to report that.

Once the Constable was long gone and out of sight, Tanguay counted another minute in her head, then headed back to her own cruiser and opened the passenger side door. She helped Dick Jeddore out of the car and to his feet.

The forestry officer was still dressed in a hospital gown under his bomber jacket, though he was also wearing his heavy hiking boots. He groaned as he stood and had to lean heavily against both the car and Marie-Ann for support. She hoped bringing him out here wasn't a bad idea.

"Did he say they've been looking all day, and no one's seen any signs of the kids?" Jeddore was breathing hard. "That's not possible. We're right between the mountain and Port Hansen, there's nowhere the kids could go."

"There were fifty volunteers out here looking this afternoon," replied Tanguay. "No one found anything."

Jeddore winced as he slipped a little on a loose rock. "I don't believe it."

"Well, come see for yourself."

She flipped on the flashlight in her left hand, using her right arm to help keep Dick upright. They stepped under the police tape and walked another few dozen meters down the road, around a bend in the trail that obscured the view of their destination from the police barricade. When they rounded the turn, Jeddore's breath caught in his throat and he gasped.

Before them, at the bottom of the steep hill, Tanguay's flashlight beam illuminated the mangled wreck of Dick Jeddore's truck. A jagged zig-zag of broken trees and turned up soil indicated the vehicle's path as it tumbled down the mountain.

Jeddore started to shudder on Tanguay's arm as if he was choking back sobs. "The kids... they walked away from this?"

"There's blood in the cab but not a lot," replied the Sergeant, trying to be as neutral as possible. She understood Jeddore's concern. The truck was crushed and folded-up like a pop can—it was inconceivable that the kids could have survived. And yet... "Seems to indicate superficial injuries. And the tracks around the vehicles suggest that all three kids climbed out of the wreckage by their own power. You can see that they circled the truck a few times, but then..."

"The tracks just stop," said Jeddore, finishing the thought. She helped him circle the wreck so he could get a good look himself, and after they made the circuit, he seemed to come to the same conclusion that everyone else had discovered earlier in the day. "It makes no sense. They just seem to vanish."

Tanguay shrugged. Her shoulder was getting tired. Jeddore was leaning on her hard, and he was not a small man. "I told you. That's what everyone who looked at the site said today."

"And you looked everywhere?"

"We had dozens of people searching. We started with a kilometre-wide radius, then expanded to three kilometres and then five kilometres. Nothing."

"What about the old military bunkers? There's a couple of them out here."

"We checked them all. We found some squatters living in one, but no sign of the kids."

Jeddore was fading fast. It seemed to take him extreme effort just to focus on the scene. He leaned against a tree to take some of the pressure off his back and groaned. "Thank you for taking me out here."

"I'm not doing it for your benefit," said Tanguay. "I hope they lock you up for child endangerment. I just want to find those kids, and if you're as good as they say you are…"

Dick waved her off. "I get it, I get it. You don't like me. But you got a soft spot for kids, huh? What's the baby shoes on the rear-view mirror about?"

Tanguay instinctively felt her hand clenched into a fist. Why had she left that there? "You mind your own business. You could be stuck in a holding cell right now with angry parents screaming at you…"

"Baby shoes," Dick said, a light going off in his head.

"Look, Jeddore, if you don't watch it…"

"No, no, baby shoes. Kids have small feet."

Dick grabbed the flashlight and headed to the mess of footprints around the wreck of the truck. They were trampled severely and rain had washed some of them away, but the small foot prints of pre-teens were clearly visible. At least for a few metres before disappearing completely.

"There were no adult footprints, right?" Jeddore asked, leaning down for a closer look. He was shaking and he could barely keep the flashlight steady.

"No, just kids."

"How many kids?"

Tanguay looked confused. "Just three."

"Did anyone count?" Jeddore asked. Tanguay shook her head, but he could tell by the look on her face that she understood. "Look, those are definitely Harper's hiking boots. And these two are sneakers, both Reeboks, one slightly smaller, that would be Pius, and the bigger one is Niall. Then who do those belong to?"

"Aren't those also sneakers?"

"Not the same as the other two. The details are blurred, but they're a different shape."

"Girls sneakers?"

"Women's. A very small ladies' shoe."

Tanguay stepped back. How was that possible? "There was a woman here?"

"Two women," Dick corrected. He pointed at another print. "That one's different, too."

"How the hell did we miss this?" Tanguay shook her head. "I've got to call this in. If there were other witnesses, we've got to find them. Dammit. Who the hell could they be?"

"I've got a pretty good guess."

Tanguay did, too, but she didn't want to say it out loud. "The woman with the red eyes?"

Jeddore nodded. "Maybe. Or maybe the women who went missing from the home."

"The grandmother? How did she get out here?"

"How did Robert Hulan get all the way up to the water supply?"

Tanguay shook her head. All of this was guesses, but it made some sense. "This is getting ridiculous. Three kids and two old women vanish into the night, plus there's a creepy old monster out there somewhere, too. How did they disappear? Did the old ladies carry them off on their brooms?"

"No, but I have another idea. I can't prove it because the prints are too washed out, but I know that Harper knows how to cover her tracks if she didn't want to be followed. She could have easily blurred her trail, especially with the rain."

"Wait, but the two women's prints disappear, too. Does that mean that they were travelling with the kids?"

"It would appear so, yes."

Well, the only good part about that would indicate that neither of the old women was the monster with the red eyes, or else the kids wouldn't have gone with them willingly. That still didn't explain where they went, though. "*Tabarnouche*. So now what?"

"Now I would appreciate it if you got me back to the hospital because I think the wound in my side is starting to bleed really bad..."

Dick removed his hand from his side, which Marie-Ann hadn't even noticed he was holding. His fingers were slick with blood.

"Crap, are you okay?" Tanguay asked.

"Probably. Maybe." He limped back toward the car. "But if I don't make it, tell them to look for another bunker."

"Another bunker? There's only two within three kilometres of here."

"There's more. There has to be. The kids didn't vanish into thin air, and there's nowhere else for them to go. They must have gone underground."

## CHAPTER SIXTEEN

*Gonna Make You Sweat*

August 23, 12:20am

Her name was Ms. Kane. The woman who was threatening them with a knife. She told them her name when she handed Skidmark a flashlight and pushed him to the front of their line. She looked a little like Skidmark's grandmother and even smelled like her. Of course, Skidmark's grandmother had never threatened anyone with a knife, at least as far as he knew, though no one would ever tell him what happened to his grandfather. The way people talked about it though, Skidmark had always assumed his grandma had done him in with a snow shovel and then dumped his body off the wharf.

They were walking down a long tunnel, somewhere under the town. After cutting off Keith's ear, the old lady had led the two boys to a drain pipe near the trailer court, just a couple of streets over from the Black Bowler and the Video Shack. The storm drain led to a secret door behind some loose stones, and then into a dizzying maze of concrete tunnels that Skidmark had no idea existed. Did anyone know these were here?

Keith had tried to escape, shortly after they had entered the tunnels. He started hyperventilating and screamed that the ceiling was coming down on them and turned to run, but Ms. Kane grabbed him by the hair and yanked him off his feet. She slashed him in the face with her knife on his way down, leaving a small but bloody gash. Had he not been falling backward at the time, the old woman probably would have taken his nose off.

Keith didn't try to escape again after that. He didn't say much either, just whimpered a lot.

Skidmark started to think Ms. Kane reminded him of the Undertaker. That guy always creeped him out whenever he showed up on Maple Leaf Wrestling on Saturday evening, with his pale face and pasty bloated manager and odd purple gloves, but Ms. Kane was even worse because she was real. It wouldn't have surprised Skidmark if she could do a Tombstone piledriver, either.

"Too slow," Ms. Kane croaked, jabbing at the two boys with her long knife. Her voice was strained and wild with a hint of instability beneath it, like Skidmark's dad when he'd been drinking. "Faster."

Keith stumbled and whimpered. Skidmark groaned. "We've been walking for an hour." He gestured down at himself. "This body is made for playing video games and building scale models of the SDF-1, not long-distance underground hiking."

"Shut up, Skidmark," muttered the old woman.

Skidmark froze, briefly, before he remembered the knife at his back. He was more than used to the nickname, even his parish priest called him Skidmark. But as far as he knew, neither he nor Keith had mentioned it in her presence. How did she know? He had no idea who she was. He had only gotten her name after prying her for fifteen minutes, and after she had threatened to cut off Keith's fingers if he hadn't shut up with the stupid questions.

"Faster," she said again, and Skidmark picked up his pace as best he could. They had made several turns in the dimly-lit, dark and dripping tunnels, the bouncing flashlight beam throwing weird shadows against the grey concrete walls. Skidmark had long ago lost track of where they were or what direction they were headed. They could be at Cape-de-Cape by now for all he knew, or even out beneath St Stephen's Bay. The thought of the ocean above their heads freaked Skidmark out considerably, and he suddenly knew how Keith felt.

Without warning, they came to a heavy, rusted metal door. Skidmark had seen enough horror movies to know that this is where they kept the flesh-eating monster, though little he imagined inside that door could be more dangerous than the freakish octogenarian with a knife and no qualms against cutting off pieces of little boys that was standing *outside* the door.

"Open it," hissed Ms. Kane.

Skidmark changed his mind. There *could* be worse things in there, he decided, and he didn't want to find out what they were.

He felt the cold prick of the knife against the back of his neck, and he changed his mind again.

The door was very heavy and stuck from age and rust. At first, Skidmark thought it was locked, but after a moment of pushing, it slowly began to creak open. It took all of his strength and several minutes to get it wide enough to reveal multiple sets of eyes staring back at him.

"Skidmark?" asked a familiar voice. "Wait, Keith? What the hell are you doing here?"

## CHAPTER SEVENTEEN

*Locked in the Trunk of a Car*

August 22, 2:15am (again)

*Twenty hours ago.*

Niall opened his eyes. He felt water dripping on his face and everything hurt. His back, his arm, his head especially. Why did he hurt so much?

The truck. Mr. Jeddore's truck. It had gone over the side of Micmac Head, with him, Pius and Harper in it.

"Pius?" he asked, still barely able to see, even with his eyes open. It was so dark. "Harper?"

He reached around and discovered he was still in the cab of the truck, laying on the underside of the roof. The truck had landed wheels up. He felt around in the dark and felt someone above him, still caught in their seat belt and dangling above his head.

Niall felt for the seat belt buckle and clicked it open, regretting it immediately. Pius' limp and heavy body felt on him, but at least from the moans, he could tell he was still alive.

"Pius!" Niall whispered. His voice was hoarse but he didn't know why. "Pius, are you okay? Where's Harper?"

"I'm here," she said, and Niall realized her voice came from outside the truck.

The door creaked open and a hand was thrust into Niall's face. His heart lifting with relief, he grabbed it and Harper helped pull him out of the truck.

For a brief moment, standing alone in the dark woods with Harper, their hands intertwined and their faces smeared with blood and dirt, Niall imagined that they were the last two people on earth, survivors of some horrible cataclysm. His mind had barely started to wander toward how they would have to repopulate the planet when Pius' moans snapped him out of his daydream.

"Am I dead? I'm dead, aren't I? Why does heaven smell like dead fish?"

Niall looked down at the remains of the truck and gasped. It barely looked like a vehicle anymore. It was just a crumpled pile of metal and glass with a few tires sticking out of it. The embankment behind showed a wide scar in the trees and ground where the truck tumbled over the side. It was a miracle they had survived this.

"You're not dead, Pius," groaned Harper. "You're in my dad's truck. Niall, help me pull him out."

Ignoring the fact that Harper was more than capable of pulling out the diminutive Pius by herself, Niall didn't argue. He wasn't going to turn down any opportunity to stand close to Harper, even if she currently smelled like blood and pee. Niall didn't actually know whose pee it was. It may have been his.

"What happened?" Pius asked when he was back on his feet and they'd convinced him that he was alive and no bones were jutting out of his body.

"The truck went over the side of the cliff, buttwipe. Are you mental?" Harper glared at her cousin.

"He did just land on his head," Niall reminded her. "We're probably all concussed."

"But how did we go over the cliff?"

"If I had crayons and construction paper, I would draw you a diagram," said Harper. "But for now, you'll just have to trust me. It looked like this."

She made a motion with her fist like an object flying through the air, then slapped her hands together to simulate the impact. She glared at him again.

Pius, with a long history of being kicked by people far meaner than Harper, ignored her. "But I mean, how did your dad go off the road? We weren't even going that fast."

"It was the woman with the red eyes," Niall spoke the words and he suddenly felt cold. He had forgotten about it until that moment when suddenly he could see her face staring at them from the middle of the road. Her burning eyes looked like they were coming from the bottom of the sea.

"The psycho hose-beast?" Harper asked.

Niall nodded. "Your dad swerved to avoid her, I saw her on the road just a second before we went over the edge."

"She's here?" Pius went paler than usual, which was especially impressive considering he was probably already in shock. "We have to get out of here."

"No," said Harper. "You get lost, or you're in trouble, you stay where you are. My dad will be here any minute looking for us anyway."

"Didn't you hear what Niall said?" said Pius, his voice rising. "She's out there! She could be coming for us any minute."

"There's something out there," said Niall.

Harper scoffed. "Don't you turn all wussy like Pius, Niall."

"No I'm serious, there's someone right over there."

Niall had caught the movement out of the corner of his eye. At first, he hoped he'd just imagined it, but now there was no denying it. There was someone standing in the trees watching them, just a few metres away. A woman.

Pius screamed. Niall, instinctively, tried to put himself in front of Harper, but Pius dove behind him and grabbed his arm, pulling him back toward the truck. Harper stepped forward defiantly.

"I don't know who you are, but stay away from us!" She pulled a small black and silver handle from her pocket and flipped open the blade of her pocket knife. She brandished it menacingly toward the woman and Niall's heart sank. It wasn't a very big knife.

The shadow woman shifted slightly but didn't respond. Niall realized suddenly that she seemed old, very old, and was bent over from age. He didn't notice the age of the woman on Micmac Head, but she definitely had a weird posture as well.

He suddenly had a horrible feeling in the pit of his stomach, like he had swallowed a bucket full of rocks and vinegar. He was going to die here. He felt cold and sick. They had survived the fall in the truck, only to be murdered by some sort of demon lady in the dark on a rainy August evening. Even dying next to Harper really did not improve his outlook on the situation. He hoped someone would feed poor Joey Smallwood.

Struck by a sudden, desperate need to do *something* in the face of his impending doom, Niall shrugged Pius off, grabbed a rock a bit smaller than his fist, and let it fly at the old woman. "Back off, you old bat!" he screamed. Since he had about as much skill with sports as he had with women, the rock went well wide.

"Niall?" asked a voice, a woman's voice, from behind them.

Niall whirled and saw another old woman, hidden in the trees. "Nana?" he asked.

Nana Josesphine Whillet emerged from the bushes. She was dressed in a pink sweat suit with black stripes down the legs and arms, and cheap Reebok sneakers. She looked like she was going for a power walk with the ladies from the Lions Club, except she was caked with dirt and leaves, and she had a wild, crazed look in her eyes.

"Niall, get down!" screamed Nana.

Without hesitating, Niall dove face-first into the mud. A split second later he heard a thump near his head as something landed beside him. He looked up into the face of the red-eyed woman, the "psycho hose-beast" as Harper called her, crouched over like an animal feeding on its prey. This was the first time he'd gotten a close look at her. Besides the fiery eyes, she was sickly and lifeless looking. Her skin was pale and sallow, like a corpse. Her gums were pulled back from her yellow teeth, making them look long and sharp. If she had once been human, she no longer was. Not for a long time.

The psycho hose-beast opened her mouth and growled, an inhuman sound like an animal. Niall had once seen a Rottweiler tear a small cat to pieces, and the sounds it made before attacking the poor feline didn't sound anything like the sound coming out of the woman now.

He wished he could hear the dying cat again. It was less terrifying.

And then suddenly there was a third old woman in the picture, the woman they had first spotted in the shadows. She looked impossibly old but she moved with a frightening speed that defied her age. She leapt between the psycho hose-beast and Niall and plunged a long, sharp knife into the growling woman's stomach. The knife piercing flesh sounded like stabbing a pumpkin with a carving knife, thought Niall.

The psycho hose-beast made a horrendous screeching sound that indicated the other woman had hit something important. The wounded woman then backed away, hissing and howling, before finally disappearing back into the forest.

There was silence for a moment, with nothing but rain pattering on the overturned truck, then Harper said: "What the heck just happened?"

Nana and Pius rushed to Niall to help him up. Miraculously, he was unhurt. Pius clutched him desperately, sobbing. "I thought you were dead. I thought she was going to strip you naked and tie you to a tree!"

"I'm fine... wait what?" That was oddly specific. "Nevermind, Nana, you're okay?"

The old woman seemed confused. She looked at Niall strangely, her head cocked to one side. "Yes, I'm fine. Who are you?"

Nana's voice sounded funny. She didn't sound like herself, and she had an accent he didn't recognize. He was used to her being confused, but the change in her voice was new.

"It's me, Nana, Niall. You just said my name, remember?"

Nana appeared to be struggling to find words. Niall looked at her and was taken aback. Since when were his Nana's eyes brown? He was sure they were grey. Maybe it was just the lighting...

The older woman interrupted his train of thought. "She's going to be back." She bent over to wipe her knife off on some leaves. "Maybe in a few hours, maybe in a few minutes. She'll need to feed, but she'll be back."

Niall suddenly realized where he recognized her from. "Holy cow, Ms. Kane. Did you both wander out of the home?"

"We didn't wander out," said Nana, still not in her own voice. She sounded more like Ms. Kane, now that he thought about it, at least she had the same accent. "We left to come find you."

"Me?" Niall was shocked. A moment ago she said she didn't know who he was.

The older woman was agitated. "No time. We go, now."

"Wait," said Harper. "Did you say that thing was going to follow us?"

"It will. Until you're dead."

"How does it hunt?"

Nana looked confused. "What do you mean?"

"I mean does it track by scent? Sound, what?"

The old woman shook her head. "In the human body, its senses are no better than a human. It can see a little better in the dark, but that's it."

Harper picked up a broken, leafy tree branch from the wreckage near the truck. "Walk in front of me."

"What are you doing?" asked Nana.

The older woman smiled. "She's covering our tracks. Clever girl."

"Actually, there's one other thing." Harper hurried to the back of the truck and fished around inside for a few moments until she came out with her dad's rifle and a box of bullets.

Ms. Kane nodded approvingly. "Very clever girl. Probably won't work, but your head's in the right place. I like this one."

They started to move away into the trees, away from the wreckage of the truck and, if Niall's guess was right, in the opposite direction of the main road. He had to drag the practically comatose Pius, who still hadn't recovered from the initial shock of the woman leaping out of the darkness. But Niall still took a moment to look back at the industrious Harper, carefully blurring their prints with her branches as they walked away from the crash site. Despite all the horror he had experienced tonight, Niall was still completely smitten with the girl.

# INTERMÈDE

*It needed to feed.*

*Just when it had started to really gain some strength—making its way out to sea for the two fools in the boat had been perhaps a bit too wasteful—that blasted human woman had set it back again.*

*It thought it would get the Hunter tonight, or at least the children. Either prize would have been a succulent feast. But all of them had gotten away. Worst, the woman's blade had bitten deep, deep enough to kill this body, under normal circumstances. Now, it had to use what little power it had just to keep the body alive.*

*If it had been strong enough, if it had just gotten another soul or two first, it would have been able to ignore any mortal weapon. But she had gotten lucky. Again.*

*It was the same woman as the last time, the one who had sealed it away sixty-three star cycles ago. She was older now, these mortals did not withstand the ravages of time very well, but it was sure it was her. It had suspected it earlier, when it saw her in the house where the mortals put their elderly to die, but now it was certain. It did, after all, have an intimate knowledge of her genetic material.*

*Just a few more, that's all it needed. One to heal the damage the old woman inflicted, another to put it back on the path of turning this frail, rotting body into something useful.*

*Somewhere in the dark, on the edge of the town, it smelled fresh food. Yes. Young, vital food. And not just one, or even two. Three. Three, unsuspecting humans, completely oblivious that they would soon become its fuel.*

*Perhaps this night would not be a total waste after all.*

## CHAPTER EIGHTEEN

*Lost Together*

August 22, 10:00pm


Niall had dreamt quite often of the first night he would spend with a girl. Harper was pretty much at the top of the list of who he wanted to spend it with, too. And yet, despite all those many, many fantasies, none of them involved spending that first night in an underground bunker. Certainly not with Pius and two crazy old ladies, one of which was his grandmother.

They were in one of the bunkers that the Americans built around the base during their time here. There were several of them, around the bay near the golf course, the matchstick factory and the fishing port, and they were all empty and left open, for anyone to explore and visit. They were just empty concrete boxes, though, so they really got boring after a few minutes. The US army had built them as bomb shelters, in case the base was ever attacked by enemy forces. But Niall had no idea that there were more of these shelters, buried deep underground, connected to the surface by a long series of concrete tunnels running under the town.

Of course, no one knew about the tunnels, either, but that was beside the point.

They were laying in the dark, on the hard, concrete floor. Harper was on one side of Niall, Pius on the other. Nana was somewhere nearby snoring softly. It was so strange—not only did she have another woman's voice and eyes, but she didn't even snore like Nana, and Niall knew his grandmother's buzzsaw-like nocturnal gargling well. He had slept over to her place many times as a kid, and Nana's snoring would keep him up at night, as well as half the neighbourhood, and caused all the dogs to bark at the horrible sound of someone stuffing a hippopotamus in a blender. People said that Nana's snoring had killed her husband, though Niall didn't understand how. Maybe it was because it kept him up every night and the chronic lack of sleep gave him a heart attack.

But this Nana—whoever she said she was—snored much more peacefully and quietly. It was so peaceful and quiet, actually, that Niall couldn't sleep. It weirded him out too much. So he stayed awake, in the dark, listening to everyone breathe and wondering what the hell he was going to do.

At least the crazy Ms. Kane was gone. Harper had begged to know if her father was alright after the crash, and she had shockingly agreed to go check on him. She seemed like a nice lady, besides blabbering about undead monsters and such. And fortunately, Nana had talked her out of taking Harper's dad's gun with her after she swore she would "blow the guts out of any bugger who got in her way." Yeah, Niall was happy she was gone. He wasn't super happy that the gun was still somewhere in this dark bunker with him and he didn't know where it was, but sometimes you had to take the lesser of two evils.

"Niall, are you awake?" Harper asked.

Niall froze. He had thought for sure she was asleep. Her breathing had been so slow, and even.

"Yeah," he answered. "How did you know?"

"You were farting a lot," she said. "I don't think people can fart like that when they're asleep."

"Of course people can fart when..." Niall realized he was raising his voice and stopped himself. He returned to a whisper. "I don't want to have this conversation."

"Well I don't want to smell it, but I guess we're all getting stuck in situations we don't enjoy."

Niall was glad Harper couldn't see his face turning red. He wanted to crawl away and beat his head against the concrete floor until the cool embrace of oblivion whisked him away from his shame, but he didn't want to wake anyone else. He was polite to a fault.

And hey, he was terrified for his life! Of course, his guts were going to be in a mess. How could she criticize...

"I hope my father's not dead," Harper said abruptly, snapping Niall out of his defensive internal monologue.

"Of course he's not," Niall said, the words sounding stupid in his own head. He didn't know. How could he know? "We survived, didn't we? I mean, I'm sure he's fine."

"If he was fine he'd be with me," she said. "Nothing in my life is fine."

Niall was hit by the crushing realization that if Mr. Jeddore was dead, that would be the second parent Harper would have lost. Crap. He hadn't fully grasped the seriousness of Harper's situation. Sure, they were all locked in an underground bunker with crazy old ladies and some kind of demon witch spawn outside their door, but if he and Pius survived, at least they would have two parents to go back to. Parents who loved them and would take care of them and maybe even be so thankful they were alive that they would buy them that Sega Genesis Mega-CD he kept hearing so much about. But there was a very good chance that Harper would have no one to go home to. Even if she survived, what would that even look like?

"I'm sorry, Harper," Niall said. He felt like maybe he should reach out and touch her, maybe hold her hand or something, but really didn't know if he should.

"Sorry for what?"

"About your parents, I mean. I know you must be freaked out."

"I am. I'm terrified that if my dad dies they might make me go live with my mom."

Niall sat up, abruptly, on one elbow. He couldn't actually see Harper in the dark, but the shock made him feel like he should somehow react physically. "Your mom? I thought your mom... I mean... I always thought..."

"That she was dead?" Harper asked. There was bitterness in her voice. Anger.

"I mean, yeah. That's what everyone thought."

"I know." She sniffled a bit. Was she crying? Niall had never heard Harper cry. In first grade Niall had seen Suzie Fowlow punch Harper in the side of the head so hard she broke her eardrum and blood poured down the side of her head but she still didn't cry. She had screamed, thrown Suzie Fowlow down and kicked her in the throat, but Harper never *cried*.

"Pius never told me," Niall said, in disbelief. "Pius tells me everything."

"Even if he knew, he might have forgotten. No one ever talks about her in my family."

Did she kill somebody? Niall almost asked, but he held his tongue. He waited for her to talk when she was ready.

"My mom had me when she was really young. Like, really young, she was still in high school. She didn't want to be a mom, but my dad didn't want to give me up. They fought over it a lot, from the bits and pieces I've heard. Dad doesn't like to talk about it. But my mom went through with it, then took off right after I was born."

"Oh my god," Niall whispered. She brushed over it, but Harper clearly said she "went through with it," which strongly implied she had considered the alternative. "I'm sorry, I didn't know..."

Niall heard her wiping her face. "It's fine. I was just worried, you know? I can't imagine going to live with her. I don't even know where she lives, for frig's sake."

The thought of Harper moving away hit Niall in the gut. He knew it was selfish, but he couldn't imagine not seeing her anymore. At least he knew she didn't want to move, either. "It will be fine. I'm sure your dad will be fine."

"You guys are too loud," Pius moaned from Niall's other side.

"Pius!" Niall said, turning back, somewhat relieved to have an excuse to get away from Harper's far-too-intense conversation. "Are you okay? You seemed really rough back there."

Niall had seen Pius break down into sobbing, nearly catatonic fits before. The last time had been when the midway amusement park rides had come to town and Niall had foolishly talked Pius into riding the roller coaster. Niall had thrown up, but Pius had been too petrified to leave his house for two days. Samantha had nearly not forgiven him.

The fact that Pius was able to form words, after an actual near-death experience, was amazing.

"I told my dad I was ashamed of him," Pius said, without emotion.

"What?"

"I told him I was ashamed of him because he didn't have a university degree," Pius explained. "That might be the last time I ever see him, and the last thing I told him was that I was embarrassed because he wasn't smart enough."

"Pius, I was there," Harper chimed in. "It wasn't like that. You didn't say you were ashamed of him."

"But he knows that's what I thought."

"Pius…" said Niall, but his best friend said nothing else. There was a long silence. "Pius?" Niall asked again but still nothing. Maybe he had fallen asleep.

"Uncle Raymond will be fine," whispered Harper. Niall realized that she had shifted closer to him, and her mouth was very close to his ear. He could feel her breath on his neck and it sent electrical charges up and down his neck so powerful that he thought for sure they would hear his heart beating in the quiet bunker. "He's got plenty of floozies to console him."

"Wait… what?" Niall was enjoying his weird little moment with Harper. Why did she have to drop a bomb like that?

"I don't think Pius knows. I don't know if Aunt Samantha knows. But I've heard him talking to my dad, and Uncle Raymond has cheated on her more than once."

Niall shook his head. Mr. Jeddore, really? On Samantha, no less? How could he do that, with such a beautiful woman at home? Niall shook his head again. And why were all of his friends' families so messed up? His family was downright boring in comparison.

"No way. With who?"

"Mrs. Dunphy, for one," said Harper.

"Mrs. Dunphy? Our English teacher?" Niall was gobsmacked. Mrs. Dunphy had one eye that was slightly lower than the other one and walked with a severe limp. She was also older than Nana.

Thinking about Nana upset Niall almost as much as thinking about Mr. Jeddore cheating on Samantha with Mrs. Dumpy Dunphy.

She should be comforting Niall in a time like this. She used to hug him when he scratched his knee or when a strange dog barked at him from across the street. But now she looked at him like she didn't know him. And not like a few days ago, when they were losing her to senility. Now she genuinely looked at him like there was a different person inside her head, a person who—while not as frightening as Ms. Kane—was still a stranger.

What would happen to Nana after this was over? If they survived whatever was out there hunting them, would Nana go back to being herself? Or to the sad old lady they brought to the home? Or would she be this strange, new person Niall didn't know? If she was, it would almost be like she was dead. Maybe worse, because there would be a person walking around that looked like Nana, but the woman that Niall knew and loved would be gone.

He couldn't say that to Harper, though. He didn't think that comparing the "deadness" of beloved relatives was appropriate for making anyone feel better.

Still, he wanted to talk to someone. About anything. Maybe she knew more about Pius' dad's dalliances.

"Harper?" Niall asked, but there was no response. She must have fallen asleep.

Niall lay alone, awake on the cold concrete floor for a long time. When he finally fell asleep, he dreamed of a time very long ago, before history, before civilization, before even dinosaurs walked the earth. He had no idea what it meant and forgot about it before he woke up.

## CHAPTER NINETEEN

*Feed My Frankenstein*

August 23; 1:10am

The other guys cheered as Steve guzzled an entire bottle of Black Horse in one go. Draining the last few drops, he roared an animalistic cry and chucked the empty bottle into the trees where it exploded with a satisfying crash.

"Eleven!" cackled Jethro, seated beside Steve on a stump, an old plaid jacket pulled right up around his ears. He was gripping his own beer in his hands. It was only his second. "You're friggin' nuts, buddy!"

Across from Jethro, the red-headed and freckled Mike shook his head. "The bet was a full dozen, Steve. You said you could down a whole dozen in under ten minutes, and you're almost out of time."

Steve pulled his last dark brown bottle out of the box by his feet, smiling broadly. He popped off the cap. "Don't you worry, boys, I got this."

He then immediately puked all over the ground, his boots, and his jeans. Jethro and Mike laughed so hard they barely had time to get out of the splash radius.

They continued to laugh so hard they didn't notice the old woman stagger out of the alder bushes, just a few paces from where they were circled around their beer boxes and empty bottles. Steve was actually the first one who noticed her, raising his head between heaves, gasping for air and contemplating how awesome this story was going to be to tell everybody next week at school. He hoped he didn't graduate again this year. Grade 12 was too awesome to give up.

"Who the hell are you?" Steve managed.

The woman was pale, and haggard, her pale skin drawn taught against her bones. She looked like a corpse and moved like one, too. She staggered and stumbled, looking drunker than Steve felt. Was she bleeding?

"Holy crap," Mike blurted out, finally noticing what was going on. "Are you alright? Do you need help?" He stood up and moved to the woman, grabbing her arm to keep her from falling.

She looked up at him. And her eyes burned like fiery coals from the pit of Hell.

Actually, to be really specific, Steve thought her eyes looked like the plastic logs in the fake fireplace his parents had in the basement. There was a flickering red light and a motor inside that made a crackling noise and produced an altogether unconvincing facsimile of burning logs. As a kid, Steve had always thought it looked weird and creepy. Now, in a walking corpse woman's face, those burning red lights looked a million times creepier.

She stared into Mike's eyes with those unnatural red lights, and the ginger-haired kid seemed transfixed, like that time he found a stack of Playboy magazines in his dad's shed. A moan escaped his lips and he began to shake like he was being electrocuted or something. Water began to pour from his nose and his mouth. The woman's gaze never broke from Mike's, and Mike seemed incapable of removing his hand from the woman's arm.

Steve took a step toward the pair but Jethro grabbed him and pulled him back. "Look at her eyes, man!" Jethro screamed. Steve had been focused on his friend, but now that he looked back he realized the woman's eyes had turned from red to blue, glowing blue, like Luke Skywalker's lightsaber. And they were getting brighter.

Mike's eyes were bloodshot and bulging out of his head, as water seeped out of his eye sockets. It was also pouring from his ears, and his flesh seemed to bubble and pulsate, like water flowing inside a waterbed. Soon the water was gushing from his mouth and nose, and even in the darkness, Steve could tell it was mixed with blood.

The more water flowed from Mike, the brighter the woman's eyes became until soon they were blinding and Steve could no longer look directly at them. He could hear, though. He could hear the sickening gurgles as Mike struggled for breath. He could hear the water splashing around his feet. And he could hear the churning of his insides as his stomach and lungs swelled up and threatened to burst.

The light from the woman's eyes exploded with a brilliant flash as bright as the sun, accompanied by a shock wave that sounded like thunder. The explosion was so powerful Steve was blown on his ass, and afterward, he could hear nothing but ringing in his ears.

Steve looked up. Mike's drowned corpse was lying at the feet of the woman. She didn't seem as pale as before, nor as bent. She was taller, stronger. And beneath her matted, stringy black hair, she was smiling.

Steve couldn't hear, but he could see Jethro running from the scene, and somehow he knew that the kid wasn't going to survive. Jethro wasn't a great runner as it was. Steve remembered they always made him play goal when they played soccer because he couldn't run for crap, not that it mattered. Steve knew at that moment that there was no escape from this creature, no matter how fast you ran. Jethro wasn't going to survive. And neither was he.

A few minutes later, with the bodies of three drowned teenage boys laying at its feet, the creature stood tall and took in its surroundings. It looked the same, and felt as strong, as it had the day it had died, 63 years earlier, under a tsunami on the other side of the island. The souls of three young men were very nourishing, much more filling than nearly dead senior citizens or even fat middle-aged fishermen. Though it would burn through their energy fast enough, it was now the strongest it had been since the storm had awoken it from its underwater prison.

It was going to enjoy its power and freedom.

# CHAPTER TWENTY

*Even Flow*

August 23; 3:25am

Skidmark took a deep breath. "So you were chased by an unkillable sea witch, rescued by two crazy old ladies, and now you're hiding under the town in a secret labyrinth of bunkers that no one has found in thirty years?"

Niall shrugged. "Yes, that's basically the gist of it. I know it's hard to believe."

"Oh, I totally believe every word you just said. I just wanted to make sure I had it all straight."

Ms. Kane had re-entered the bunker a few minutes ago with Brian Hawco and Keith Doucette, for some reason, joining Niall, Harper, Pius and Nana Josephine in the small, tomb-like cement enclosure. They were deep underground, very deep, as best Brian could tell, lit only by a couple of flashlights and a small flickering propane camp lantern the old women had brought with them. The walls and ceiling above them felt so heavy, so oppressive, Niall could nearly feel the weight of the concrete in the very air. He wasn't claustrophobic, but even he had a little difficulty breathing. Poor Pius was a gibbering mess on the floor in the corner. Even more than usual.

Skidmark scratched the back of his neck, looking some combination of embarrassed and humbled. "I'm just wondering why you asked the crazy old lady to come get me, of all people."

"Her name is Ms. Kane," snapped Harper.

"We've been in here all day," explained Niall. "And we have no idea what's going on outside. Nana and Ms. Kane told us it wasn't safe for any of us to leave, so we sent her to go find Harper's dad. When she couldn't find him, we thought of the only other person who might believe us about all the weird stuff that was happening in town."

"I have been trudging all over and under this town for hours," grumbled Ms. Kane. "Do you know how hard that is for an old woman like me? I've got bunions bigger than your testicles, boy."

No one was really sure who Ms. Kane was talking about, so they just continued on uncomfortably. "So we need you..."

"What the hell is going on here, anyway?" Keith demanded. He had been silent since they entered the room, quietly seething near the door, but now his anger bubbled up to the surface. "When I get out of here, I'm going to tell my dad to call the cops—"

"Ugh, who brought him, anyway?" groaned Harper.

"You said no witnesses," said Ms. Kane, casually brandishing her knife. "It was either kill him or take him with us."

Harper rolled her eyes. "You should have killed him. It really wouldn't have been any loss."

Keith, who's hair was caked with blood and appeared to be missing part of an ear, seemed to be spoiling for a fight. He lunged at Harper. "You bitch, I'm going to kill you..."

"No one's killing anyone!" snapped Nana Josephine. Keith froze, as did everyone else in the bunker besides Ms. Kane, who spat on the floor and giggled. It was still weird hearing another woman's voice come out of Nana's mouth, but Niall was thankful that it was powerful enough that it was impossible to ignore. "There are enough people dying out there now! If we can help it, we're going to stop the killing. Somehow."

Niall sighed. "Keith, I'm sorry you got caught up in this. I guess if you want to go you can, but it is really dangerous out there."

"No." Nana Josephine's voice was firm and unwavering. Niall couldn't believe this was the same woman they had dropped off at the home a couple of days ago. Not only was she clear-headed, but she also had the energy and vitality of a woman twenty years younger. And, you know, she sounded like Natasha from those old Rocky and Bullwinkle cartoons. "I'm sorry son, but you can't leave. It's too risky."

"I say let him go!" insisted Harper. "Let the psycho hose-beast eat him!"

"Unfortunately, Ethelinda is right," sighed Ms. Kane. "If the creature absorbs Keith it will only grow stronger. Best we just slit his throat ourselves and get it over with."

Keith recoiled, pressing himself against the bare concrete wall. "Get the hell away from me, you crazy hag!"

"No one is killing anyone!" snapped Josephine.

"And who the heck is Ethelinda?" asked Harper.

Niall had caught that too. Who was Ms. Kane talking about?

"We should tell them the rest of the story," said Nana Josephine.

"Fine."

"I love stories," said Skidmark, sitting down cross-legged in front of the crone like a kid in kindergarten in front of his teacher.

"My name isn't Ms. Kane," began the old woman. "I was born Theolina Benoit, in a small village in the Burin Peninsula. My family were outcasts, as my father was an Indian and my mother was a gypsy."

"My dad has names for people like you," said Keith.

"I trust you to keep them to yourself or I'll make your tongue match your ear." Ms. Kane—Ms. Benoit, Niall reminded himself—flicked her blade toward Keith. "I had a twin sister. We grew up both shunned and sought out by our community. Shunned because of who our parents were. And sought out for the healing and succour we could bring.

"You were witches!" Skidmark's eyes lit up. Niall had already heard this part of the story and he had a hard time believing it, too. "Not like *Wizard of Oz*, ruby-slipper-stealing, flying monkey-leading witches, but more like *Kiki's Delivery Service*, making potions and helping-the-community witches."

"Just ignore him," said Harper, picking up on the old woman's blank face. "Everyone does."

"It's true," said Skidmark. "My mom once forgot to feed me for three days."

Theolina Benoit shook her head. "Some people called us witches. I think we just helped women deliver babies and cured stomach pains and pulled abscessed teeth. The only magic we ever tried was to stop a great and powerful evil, which was released from its underwater prison by a great undersea earthquake."

"Did it work?" asked Niall.

Theolina nodded. "It did, yes. But many people lost their lives that day, including my sister."

"I'm not dead," grumbled Nana Josephine.

The older lady smiled and crossed her spindly arms. "You've been dead for over sixty years, and you know it's true."

"I can't be. I'm here, aren't I?"

"What's going on?" asked Harper.

Nana sighed. "I'm Ethelinda Benoit, her sister."

"No, you're not," said Niall. "You're my Nana Josephine Whillet."

"You're both, technically, right," said Theolina, a wicked, lopsided grin on her face.

"So cool," whispered Skidmark.

"It's nonsense," scoffed Nana. "You can't be in two places at once, Theolina, nor in two people for that matter."

Something clicked in Niall's mind. Something about someone being "in" someone. "Ms. Kane, er Benoit, did you have an Uncle Archie? Who owned a bunch of animals?"

"I did indeed," answered Theolina Benoit, looking at Niall carefully. She had a sour face and deep, probing gaze. She would have been a great teacher; he felt like he was being tested. "And how do you know this, young man?"

Both old women now stared at him, Nana with as much intensity as old Ms. Kane/Benoit. Niall had never seen that look on Nana's face. She looked like she *wanted* him to screw up and say something stupid, so she could jump on him and tell him he was wrong. Oddly, that reminded him of several teachers he'd had, too.

Even stranger, it was Keith who saved him, though it was completely unintentional.

Niall heard a strange humming noise bubbling up behind the old women, and both of them whipped around at the same time. Keith, who had been leaning against the wall with his hands in the pockets of his shorts, was singing softly to himself but stopped mid-note when the old ladies turned on him.

"What are you doing?" demanded Theolina, fury rising in her voice. Keith might as well have been perpetrating the worst crimes imaginable, like passing notes with "do you like me" check boxes, or chewing gum in class and sticking it on the bottom of his desk.

"It's 'Achy Breaky Heart,' by Billy Ray Cyrus," Keith said, dumbly.

"No singing!" hissed Nana, in a voice that terrified Niall. For a moment she sounded more like an animal than a human. "We hates it!"

"To be fair, it's not even really a song," said Harper.

"You shut your filthy mouth!" spat Keith.

"The creature out there," Theolina pointed in the vague, general direction of the world above them. "The one Harper so eloquently calls the 'Psycho Hose-Beast,' is highly susceptible to noise, and especially music. Some tunes will calm it, others will enrage it. Either way, any song, regardless of its musical merit, could attract its attention."

Skidmark raised his hand. Theolina looked at Nana, then Niall, who shrugged. "Yes, boy?"

"The Psycho Hose-Beast, is that the evil you tried to stop all those years ago?"

Theolina nodded.

"Cool!" exclaimed Skidmark

"It's also my sister, Ethelinda."

"You lost me," said Keith.

Niall was confused, too, and they had already explained most of this to him. "That creature, your Psycho Hose-Beast, has taken over my dead sister's body..."

"I'm right here, you twit," grumbled Nana.

"...her *original* body," Theolina corrected. "Ethelinda gave up her life to stop it, and it somehow ended up possessing her."

"That is messed up," giggled Skidmark.

"But then where has it been for the last sixty years?" asked Harper.

"Presumably at the bottom of the Atlantic," replied Theolina.

"I call bullshit on that one," said Keith. "How can an old lady live on the bottom of the sea for a million years?"

"Nobody asked you," snapped Harper.

"It's because she's possessed by a demon, duh," said Skidmark. He looked incredibly pleased with himself. "And the storm this weekend released it from whatever was trapping it, right? Do I have it right? And was it a demon? Devil? Alien? Extra-dimensional alien? Great old one? Ghost? Spirit of nature? Fairy?"

Theolina smiled. "Something like that."

Skidmark opened his mouth and closed it again, possibly the first time Niall had ever seen him at a loss for words. "How do we stop it?"

"Stop it?" a voice came up from somewhere at the back of the room. "We?"

All eyes turned to Pius, who was curled up in a corner. He looked a wreck, drenched in sweat and with eyes red and sunken. It was the first words he had spoken in hours. "Why do *we* have to do anything? We're just a bunch of kids. There's a monster out there killing people. We should be calling the cops or the military or someone to deal with this!"

"He's right," said Nana Josephine. She turned to Theolina. "They are just children. They should stay here where it's safe..."

Theolina cackled. "Safe? Nowhere is safe. The being that inhabits your old body gets stronger with every life it takes. It has killed how many already? Four, that we know of? In just one night? It may have killed a dozen more while we've been hiding here. Soon it will have enough power that we won't be able to stop it. If we don't act soon there will be no point in having this conversation, because it will be unkillable. And it won't stop feeding until it devours all the life on this world."

Nana sighed. "If it's already consumed the Hunter, it may be too late."

"No," said Theolina. "There is another option."

Josephine glared at Theolina and hissed under her breath. She glanced furtively at Harper, but Niall caught it, mostly because he always had one eye on Harper. Harper noticed it, too.

"What are you talking about?" she asked. "Who's the 'Hunter?'"

"Nothing for you to worry about, dear." Josephine put her hand on Harper's shoulder. "And there is no need to scare these children further."

"I'm not scared!" squealed Skidmark. "This is awesome! This is like we're in a horror movie! Or Star Trek!"

"I don't understand half of what comes out of that boy's mouth," said Josephine, shaking her head at Skidmark. "But even if he's soft in the head, there's no need to be dragging them into this."

Was it true? It was all so crazy. Body swapping, monsters from beneath the sea, magic. It couldn't be true, could it? But Niall had seen the red-eyed creature himself. He had seen the lightning and Harper and Pius had seen the dead woman in the tree. There was something extremely weird going on. How else could he explain it?

Niall suddenly noticed a strange tingling at the base of his neck. First, he just thought it was an itch, but it was deeper than that. It felt like warmth, deep inside him. The bunker was so cold and damp, he hadn't felt anything warm like this in hours.

He closed his eyes and realized he could still see the inside of the bunker perfectly. It was disorienting. Had he been staring at these walls so long they were burned in the inside of his eyelids? Like that time he played *Super Adventure Island* for 16 hours straight and then dreamed about it for a week?

Niall opened his eyes, and there were the bunker walls again. Except no, they weren't. He closed his eyes and sure enough, what he was seeing in his head wasn't the bunker they were hiding in. It was the tunnels outside. And they were moving. Well, he was moving, in his vision, travelling down the dark grey concrete corridors, heading towards... where was he going?

*Food. He was going to feed.*

Oh no. No, no, no. This wasn't possible. Out of the corner of his mind's eye he caught a reflection in a dark puddle. A reflection of a woman in a torn, rotten dress. With glowing red eyes.

Niall opened *his* eyes. It took him a moment to realize that yes, this was the real world, that he was in his own body in the here and now. But that other world, that vision, was equally real, not like his daydreams of listening to Dream Theater cassette tapes with Cindy Crawford.

"She's coming!" Niall blurted out, before his conscious mind even registered what he was talking about. All eyes in the room stopped and turned toward him.

There was a heavy bang on the rusted metal door.

# CHAPTER TWENTY-ONE

*Don't Cry*

August 23, 3:20am


Marie-Ann Tanguay sat at her desk, trying to make sense of it all.

Four dead bodies, all apparently drowned in sea water, only two of which were actually found near the ocean. One of the dead was a blind senior citizen who lived in the retirement home where there were now two more missing seniors. Three missing kids, one of which had a connection to the senior's home, as his grandmother was one of the missing old women. The other two kids were related to Dick Jeddore, the Fisheries and Wildlife officer who was now lying in Sir Wilfred Grenfell Hospital in serious condition after driving his truck off a cliff on Micmac Head. Dick Jeddore, who had had at least two encounters with a mysterious red-eyed woman.

There had been two more eyewitness reports of the red-eyed woman. A janitor saw her at the senior's home the night Robert Hulan disappeared, and one of Mrs. Noseworthy's neighbours reported seeing her the night the old lady ended up swinging naked from the trees in her backyard. Plus, Dick said the kids had seen her, too.

It was the kids that worried Marie-Ann the most. Whether or not there was a monstrous murderer stalking the town, she had to make sure the kids were okay. There were over fifty people scouring the town for them, surely they had to show up somewhere. She even had Constables Bennett and Brake out scouring Micmac Head in the dead of night, looking for another bunker. It was all crazy, but what else could she do?

She had contacted her superiors about getting backup, but every RCMP detachment on the West Coast of the island had been dealing with fall-out from the storm. It was bad enough they had to spare forensic investigators for a few drowned seniors and fishermen, but there was no way she was getting help for a few missing kids. Unless she was willing to officially call this a homicide investigation, she was on her own for now.

She was staring at the framed baby picture on her desk when Constable Cheryl Murphy appeared at the door. Marie-Ann nearly jumped out of her chair, surprised that there was anyone else in the station at this hour. "Excuse me, sergeant," the round, usually jovial woman said, her voice uncharacteristically subdued. "I was just about to boil the kettle, would you like a tea?"

"What are you doing here so late?"

"I always like to stay near the radio when we've got boys out in the field," responded Murphy, referring to Bennett and Brake. Marie-Ann hadn't ordered her to be on duty; usually, if there was no one in the office the calls would be put through to the nearest detachment that did have someone on shift, but Cheryl Murphy was like a mother hen, always fussing about her fellow officers, worrying about them and taking care of them. That's why she was offering the sergeant a cup of tea at half-past three in the morning.

Marie-Ann usually drank coffee and was about to decline when she stopped herself. Constable Murphy knew she didn't drink tea. The woman was trying to provide comfort to her obviously-stressed CO. Marie-Ann never opened herself up much to the other staff at any of her postings, and she certainly hadn't since transferring here just a few months ago. But right now, maybe she needed to hear another voice just to get her out of her own head.

The sergeant sighed. "You know what? Yes, please. I'll have a cup of tea."

Constable Murphy stared as if the sergeant had slapped a freshly-bludgeoned seal pup on her desk. "Oh, of course. Right away." She ran off a moment, then ducked her head back in. "How do you take it? Cream? Sugar?"

"Just milk, thank you."

"Such a shame about those kids," Murphy called from the other room as she busied about making the tea. "Still no leads?"

"Nothing. At least nothing concrete. We've scoured every centimetre of those woods and bog three times over. We're going to have to call in someone to dredge Mine Pond tomorrow if nothing else turns up soon."

"Oh dear," Murphy said, coming in with a steaming cup of tea, which she placed carefully on the sergeant's desk. "Sorry, I don't think I've ever asked you. Do you have any kids, Sergeant?

"No."

Murphy's eyes darted to the baby picture on the desk, but she said nothing. Marie-Ann cursed herself for leaving it out in the open. Murphy cleared her throat. "I have two little ones myself. Two girls. I know I would be beside myself if something happened to them. I can't imagine what Mrs. O'Neill is going through, with both her son and her mother missing like that."

Tanguay nodded. She would have to question Barbara O'Neill at some point. She hated harassing the woman in what was surely a difficult time for her family, but it was awfully strange that both her son and mother went missing at the same time. Not suspicious, necessarily, but strange.

The radio on her desk crackled to life and Tanguay jumped to answer it. "Bennett?"

"Yeah, Sarge. We found..."

For the briefest moment, Marie-Ann's heart leapt. "You found the kids?"

"Not the kids we were looking for. You were right, we found another bunker. And there were kids inside, not as young as the ones that were missing, but... I don't want to say it on the radio."

No. "Dammit, Bennett. Is it the same cause of death?"

There was a pause. "Yes."

*Tabernac.* Three more. Kids this time.

She was already on her feet and heading for the door, radio in hand. Constable Murphy briefly lifted her tea toward her, but then put it back on the desk. "I'm coming, Bennett, where are you?"

"On the other side of Mine Pond. I'll meet you at the road."


Marie-Ann was somewhat relieved when she saw the bodies.

They were kids, but barely. Young men, really, at least seventeen, eighteen years old. Still a tragedy, but at least they weren't little kids. She wasn't sure if she would be able to handle finding that. There were three of them, all drowned and still soaking wet with salt water. Bennett and Brake had cordoned off the crime scene, and the very busy local EMTs were already dealing with the body. They were all in a concrete bunker, hidden away beneath the bog at the foot of Micmac Head. The place was dry, and still, and probably hadn't been opened in over 30 years.

The place gave Tanguay the creeps. She stepped outside and gestured for Bennett to follow her. "Tell me everything."

"We started looking for more bunkers, like you said. A couple of the volunteers found this one, but we probably never would have noticed it except that it had been opened recently."

"By whoever put the bodies here," said Tanguay.

"You don't think the kids died inside?"

Tanguay glared at him. "Seriously? You think the three of them drowned in a bone dry, empty bunker?"

"Stranger things have happened," suggested Bennett.

That much was true. It had been a screwed-up week.

"We can see the drag marks where they brought the bodies in," Tanguay gestured to the ground around the moss-and-sod covered door of the previously-hidden bunker. "Why don't I see any marks coming out?"

"We don't think there was."

"Was there anyone else in there?"

"No, but there is another door."

Marie-Ann wanted to slap the constable's dumb hairy face, like his mother should have done more often. "You couldn't have led with that?" she marched back in the bunker and sure enough, there was a heavy iron door at the far end. Marks on the ground even indicated it had been recently opened.

She grabbed the handle and pulled, but the door didn't budge. She tried to push to the same result.

"We tried that," said Bennett. "Seems like it's locked."

"And you didn't think to mention it?"

"Well we can't open it, so it wasn't pressing."

"There could be a serial killer on the other side of this door, and you didn't think it was pressing?"

"It's probably another sealed, enclosed shelter. There's no way to get out of here."

Tanguay grabbed her radio and called dispatch. "Cheryl, get me a locksmith and a welder. And get every available officer down here now."

A few hours later, when the metal door had been cut away and opened, it revealed a long, dark staircase disappearing into the ground.

Tanguay glared at Bennett, who at least at the decency to look embarrassed.

"Dumbass," she muttered.

# CHAPTER TWENTY-TWO

*Symphony of Destruction*

August 23, 3:50am

"What do we do?" screamed Harper. "What do we do? What do we do?"

"Let it come." Theolina cocked the bolt of Harper's rifle and smiled.

"You are a ninety-year-old woman!" Niall reminded her. "You are not Rambo!"

"She knows we can't kill it, she just wants to shoot something," said Nana Josephine. "But she has a point. The only way out is through that door. We have to open it."

"I am quite happy to just stay inside here and wait it out," said Keith.

The pounding on the door was getting more fierce. Gravel and dirt fell from the walls and ceiling.

Niall knew they were trapped. He had walked through the bunker several times in the long hours they'd spent here, and there was no other way out. Still, the door was solid metal. There was no way the creature could get through, was there?

More dirt and rubble crumbled around the door frame. The metal squealed teeth-shatteringly as something tore into it on the other side.

"It won't hold forever," said Nana Josephine, dashing the rest of Niall's hopes.

"We let it in," Theolina said again. "We take it now, we have surprise on our side. If we leave it alone, it's going to be angrier when it eventually gets through. Besides, we can hurt it now. If we wait for it to get more powerful, we don't have that option."

"You know we can't kill it yet," Nana Josephine reminded her again. "We need—"

"I know what we need!" the older woman snapped. "But a bullet between the eyes should slow it down, right? Plus the blood will look so pretty, splattered on the wall."

Everyone was so horrified by Theolina's words, no one was paying attention to Skidmark until it was too late. He grabbed the latch and pulled it open. Harper screamed at him.

"What?" he asked. "I was always told to listen to my elders."

Keith, closest to the door, moved to lock it again, but it was too late. The door flew open and the Psycho Hose Beast burst into the room.

It looked a bit like Theolina, but younger and older at the same time. Younger because the woman's body was probably no more than twenty years old, older because it looked like it had spent fifty years on the body of the ocean. Still, it looked healthier than it had when they saw it last. Less pale and skeletal. Was it indeed getting stronger?

The creature made a beeline for Theolina. The old woman got off a shot but it went wide, and the echo of the blast made Niall think his eardrums had popped. He had never heard anything so loud.

Head and ears ringing, Niall looked up to see the Psycho Hose Beast perched on top of Theolina, clawing and biting at her face. The old woman used the rifle to hold her back, but by using it as a shield she had no chance to reload it.

"Get it off of her!" Nana Josephine screamed.

"I'm not touching it!" howled Keith.

"Distract it!" cried Theolina. "I need to reload the gun!"

"I'm still not touching it!"

Niall glanced frantically around the floor. He needed something—a rock, a weapon, anything. He grabbed one of the cheap flashlights and hurled it at the creature. It bounced harmlessly off its back and shattered `on the ground, leaving the bunker that much darker.

He could run. The door was open now, and the monster was distracted with the crazy old woman. He could grab Harper's hand and they could escape, if they could navigate their way through the labyrinthine maze of tunnels beneath the town. He couldn't leave Pius though, who was still a useless mess of drool in the corner.

Then he heard it. At first he couldn't believe it, thought for sure he was hearing things. But then the sound drifted up, as unmistakable as a loud wet fart in a quiet elevator, somehow rising above the snarls and growls of the horrific woman trying to eat Theolina Benoit.

*"Informer - You no say Daddy me Snow me, I'll go blame - A licky boom-boom down..."*

All eyes in the bunker, including the red glowing eyes of the creature, turned toward Skidmark.

The small round boy was bobbing up and down, strutting and rolling his best rapper moves. Either that, or he was having some sort of seizure. Niall was genuinely afraid for his health.

"'Tective man says Daddy me Snow me stabbed someone down the lane - A licky boom-boom down..."

"What the frig are you doing?" hissed Keith.

Skidmark ignored him. He continued bouncing his head up and down to the imaginary music that only he could hear. Well, to be honest Niall could hear it, too. That song was everywhere these days, and once you got it in your head you couldn't really do anything about it.

"Informer - You no say Daddy me Snow me, I'll go blame - A licky boom-boom down..."

It was working. The Psycho Hose Beast rose from its position atop Theolina, turning its full attention toward Skidmark's surprisingly competent rapping. The creature approached him, moving slowly, its human head bobbing and twitching in time to the music like a confused dog trying to make sense of its prey.

"Police-a them-a they come and-a they blow down me door - One him come crawl through through my window..."

It drew closer and closer. Skidmark backed up nearly flat against the concrete wall of the bunker, but he kept singing.

"So they put me in the back the car at the station - From that point on I reach my destination..."

The Psycho Hose Beast opened its mouth, bared its yellow teeth, blood and spittle dripping from its salt-water-smelling maw. And then the room exploded again with another deafening gunshot. Blood burst from the side of the creature's neck, splattering Skidmark and cutting his tune off mid-syllable. The creature slumped to its knees, revealing Harper behind it, holding the smoking rifle.

"What took you so long?" asked Skidmark.

"Sorry, I had to get the bullets from Theolina," Harper replied, ejecting the spent casing and reloading it in a smooth, practiced motion. Without another word, she raised the gun and fired another round into the Psycho Hose Beast, this one right between its shoulder blades. This time it fell to the floor, but it was still moving, and trying to get up.

"Goddamn that's loud!" screamed Keith, holding his ears. "It's only a .22, why is it so loud? Can you stop doing that!"

"I'll stop when that whack thing stops moving!" She reloaded and fired again, and the insides of Niall's ears felt like goo. How the heck did that guy in Wolfenstein 3D run around through basements and tunnels all the time blasting stuff with machine guns? He must have been completely deaf.

"You can't kill it with bullets!" screamed Theolina. All of them were yelling at the top of their lungs now, their hearing totally cocked up. "We have to go, now!"

"This was your idea!" Niall screamed back at her.

"I told you it wasn't going to kill it!"

Keith shook his fists in frustration. "Make up your friggin' mind, old woman!"

Harper raised the gun again, but sighed and lowered it. The creature was already rising back onto its hands and feet. "I have to get to my dad," she yelled.

"We can get to the hospital through the tunnels," said Theolina. "I'll show you the way!"

"What about her?" Niall asked, shocking himself with his practicality in the situation. But if Harper was going to be a badass with a gun and Skidmark was saving them with his white boy rapping, he figured he would have to find a way to make himself useful, too. "We should warn the authorities!"

"What are they going to do?" asked Harper. "This obviously doesn't work."

She unloaded another round in the Psycho Hose Beast, spraying more blood on the concrete and causing everyone to scream in shock and pain, but it continued trying to stand up.

"Stop doing that!" screamed Keith.

"We need to warn other people to be careful!" said Niall. "We should tell the cops!"

"Go, then!" said Theolina. "It's a straight line to the police station from here!"

"What about Pius?" asked Niall. "I don't know if he can walk."

Keith shouldered past Niall and headed for the boy in the corner. "I will carry the bastard and go with you if it means I can get away from that crazy chick with the gun!"

Keith hefted Pius up onto his shoulders, and the smaller boy did not protest.

As the groups were separating at the door, Niall had deep reservations about his choice. Sure, it would bring him to the police station and potentially armed protection, but it was also bringing him away from Harper. That had been a poor decision on his part.

"Hey, Skidmark," said Keith, as they were on their way out. "That was actually pretty cool."

"Thanks! I also know all the words to Vanilla Ice's Ninja Rap."

"Wicked." Keith nodded and headed off.

"You be careful!" Niall told Harper. Surprising himself, he awkwardly placed a hand on her shoulder. The tips of his fingers tingled at the touch of her t-shirt.

"You too," she said. She took his hand in hers, moved it away from her shoulder, and squeezed it. She gave him a slight smile that could have meant a million things, then turned and hurried off down the corridor with the two old women and Skidmark.

Niall watched them go for a long moment, confused by a thousand emotions welling up inside his chest. What did that hand squeeze mean? What did that smile mean? And would he ever even see her again?

The creature moaned and stirred inside the room, snapping Niall back into reality. He slammed the door to the bunker and ran off the opposite way down the corridor after Keith and Pius.

## INTERMÈDE

*That really hurt.*

*It was not used to wounds like this. It had suffered injury before, sure, but not so many grievous wounds so quickly. These... guns the mortals had invented were truly armaments of the damned. And they called it the monster?*

*Humans were the true monsters. They would need to be wiped out. Quickly.*

*But it had lost so much strength. The energy from the youths in the forest had nearly restored its mortal shell completely, but that had been the mistake. What did a being from the Primordial Dawn of Time need with a mortal shell? Looking like a human had made it think like a human, and so it didn't use the best weapons it had at its disposal. It had the witch at its mercy and it didn't finish her off. It would not make that mistake again.*

*It needed a body, sure, in order to destroy those wretched humans, but it didn't need to look like anything human. The time for subtlety had passed.*

*Now it just needed a little more power, just a little, to start knitting itself back together...*

*It took far more strength than it would have liked, to open the heavy metal door, where it found itself with two paths to take. The humans had split up. Interesting. There was something about the boy with the yellow hair, something it could not yet figure out, but the witch went with the girl and the gun. There was something about the girl with the gun. Something about her smell. Yes, it knew who she was, and where it was probably going.*

*And now it knew where to go.*

## CHAPTER TWENTY-THREE

*Jeremy*

August 23, 6:10am

Marie-Ann Tanguay came back to the detachment, tired and exhausted, wondering if Cheryl could make her another cup of tea. Scratch that, this time she would ask for coffee. Or maybe even a shot of whiskey. The previous sergeant had apparently left bottles of booze hidden all over the building, she just needed to find one.

She was so tired and lost in her own thoughts that Marie-Ann nearly ran headlong into Cheryl when she walked in through the door.

"Oh my dear, you're going to want to see this," was all the Constable could say, then led her to her office.

There were three boys sitting in her office, all between the ages of twelve and fourteen. She recognized two of them as the missing O'Neill and Jeddore kids. She actually recognized the third one, too. It was the big kid on the expensive bike, the one that had been threatening to beat up the Jeddore boy a few days ago. What were they doing together now? And how the hell did they get back here? They were all dirty and looked tired, and the bully had blood in his hair and appeared to be missing part of his ear, but they were alive.

"What the hell?" was all Tanguay could manage.

"They came in just a couple of minutes ago, I didn't even get a chance to call you yet," Cheryl explained. "They wouldn't tell me what's been going on."

"Boys," Tanguay said, wondering where to start. "A lot of people have been worried about you, and looking for you."

"Even me?" asked the bully kid.

"No, I don't even know who you are," replied Marie-Ann. The big kid's face fell. "But the rest of you—Pius, Niall? Are you okay? Where is the girl, Harper?"

"She's fine," said Niall O'Neill. "Or she was when we left her a little while ago. She was on her way to the hospital to check on her dad."

Had they just been hiding for the last two days? It seemed impossible. "What happened to you? Where have you been?"

"It's kinda hard to explain," said Niall.

"Try me."

"There's a crazy psycho witch lady," added Keith. He pointed at the wound on his head. "She cut my ear off. There's also a Psycho Hose Beast that came from the bottom of the sea. Or maybe outer space, I don't know."

"I believe you."

Niall and Keith looked shocked. They looked at each other, then back at Marie-Ann. "You do?"

"I know something strange is going on here. I want answers. Tell me everything that happened to you and what you know."

She knew she should wait for the kids' parents to get here before talking to them, but she couldn't wait. This craziness had been going on too long, and she had to get something, some kind of answer, as quickly as possible. Waiting for the parents to show up, and then sitting through their tearful reunions, would waste time. Time that more people could die. Two of the missing kids were in front of her right now. She had to make sure the third one was okay, too.

So Niall told her about waking up after falling over Micmac Head. He told her that they met the red-eyed creature before being rescued by two old ladies—Ms. Kane and Josephine Whillet. Except they didn't call themselves that anymore—they called themselves Ethelinda and Theolina Benoit.

"I've heard those names before," Tanguay said, taking notes as Niall explained it. "Harper's Dad told them to me, too. I looked them up in all the RCMP records and I can't find them anywhere."

"Nana wasn't talking like herself at all, and she was talking about places and people she shouldn't know."

"Tell her how she sent the other one to come cut my ear off," said Keith.

Niall went on, about how they hid out in tunnels under the town, tunnels that must have been connected to the bunker they found earlier that day near Mine Pond. The old ladies kept telling them that the monster was going to go after Harper's dad, so they sent Theolina to look for him, but she didn't know he was in the hospital. So she took Keith and another kid to try and get information. But then the monster showed up again and everything went to hell.

Tanguay was especially disconcerted about the part where the Jeddore girl shot the so-called "Psycho Hose Beast" a half-dozen times with a hunting rifle and she kept getting back up. She really hoped the kids were mistaken, or exaggerating.

"Cheryl, call Constable Squires, he's at the hospital watching Jeddore. Tell him that the girl and the two missing women from the seniors home could be showing up at any time. Tell him to make sure they don't leave!"

The other woman nodded and hurried back to her station.

"We need to check on Harper and Skidmark, I mean, Brian," said Niall.

"They'll be fine," Tanguay assured him. "Do you guys really call him 'Skidmark?' He's okay with that?"

Keith shrugged. "It suits him much better than Brian. Wait'll you see him yourself."

"You kids will wait here until your parents get down here."

"We can't just wait around," objected Niall. "That monster is out there, and it gets more powerful the more people it kills! Everyone in town is in danger!"

"What am I supposed to do, call in a SWAT team?"

"Yes!" retorted Niall.

"That sounds like a good idea," agreed Keith.

"Call in an airstrike, call in the army, do whatever you have to do!" Niall pleaded.

"Niall, I know this is upsetting, and I believe you, I really do. I just can't call my superiors and tell them there's a red-eyed lady running around magically killing people with salt water! What am I supposed to tell them?"

"Tell them there's a mass murderer on the loose. Won't that bring you reinforcements?"

"Yes, but it will be reinforcements looking for a man. According to you, that won't work."

"We have to try something!"

"Then give me something! Anything! What are we dealing with? I don't even have a name besides a couple of made-up sounding Benoits that don't even seem to exist."

"You're looking in the wrong place."

The voice was weak. It came from the Jeddore kid, the one who looked sick and hadn't spoken yet. "Excuse me?" asked Tanguay.

"Pius, are you okay?" asked Niall.

"You're looking in the wrong place. You checked the RCMP records, but they'll only go back as far as 1949, since Newfoundland's been part of Canada. Theolina and Niall's Nana mentioned Kelly's Island several times, talking about when they were kids. That must have been at least fifty or sixty years ago."

"So you're saying we need to look up information on Kelly's Island from before 1949?" scoffed Tanguay. "And where do you propose we do that?"

Pius managed a weak smile. "We need to go to the library."

## CHAPTER TWENTY-FOUR

*Man in the Box*

August 23, 7:05am

Sir Wilfred Grenfell Hospital was built at one of the highest points in town, overlooking the sprawling hamlet of Gale Harbour. It had been constructed by the US Military during the war years when it had probably been state-of-the-art for its time. Now, not so much.

Brian hated the hospital. It looked run-down, with faded paint on the walls and floors lined with linoleum that was probably older than his grandmother. Not to mention all the asbestos that was assuredly stuffed in the ceilings and floating in the air. Brian always thought the hospital smelled like death. Now, after having actually seen and smelled dead bodies, he realized that the smell was actually the awful industrial cleaning supplies they used here. He had just associated it with death because the only time his parents brought him here was to visit dying relatives.

The four of them—Skidmark, Harper, and the two old ladies that didn't even seem to know their own names, so why would Brian be expected to remember them—emerged from the tunnels in an old boiler room deep beneath the hospital. Mice scattered as the heavy door opened for the first time in decades. It had been forgotten behind a pile of ancient, rotting shipping palettes, which they had to move out of the way to get into the basement proper and into the rest of the hospital. Actually Harper had moved most of the wood by herself, seeing as she was the only one who wasn't decrepit or Skidmark.

"Why did you bring me again?" asked Brian, a perfectly honest question. They were creeping up an old set of stairs to the main floor of the hospital.

"I just wanted to know where my dad was," said Harper. "Now that we know I suppose you can leave."

Brian thought about it. "If it's all the same I think I'll stick around a little longer," he said. "I mean, I kinda want to see how this all turns out. Plus, you need me! Who else knows all the words to every 3rd Bass song?"

"Just because that worked once doesn't mean it will work again," groaned Harper.

"Actually, it really hates music," said Nana Josephine-Ethelinda. "It probably would work again, though it would likely just make her kill the boy faster."

Harper looked like she didn't think that was a loss, but she did relent. "Fine. But could you sing some Tori Amos instead?"

"Who?" asked Brian.

"Quiet," Theolina hissed from the top of the stairs. For a woman who was pushing ninety, she was awfully spry. She had been going non-stop since kidnapping Keith and Brian last night, and she was still taking the stairs two at a time. Brian was doing one at a time and still had to stop to catch his breath after every fourth or fifth step.

The old woman gestured for them to keep it down. The door was cracked open and she watched a few people walk past, then ushered everyone through.

"Act casual," whispered Theolina as the group started to walk down the grotesquely off-white coloured hallway.

"Casual? We're covered in blood!" Harper reminded her.

"Yes, but it is a hospital. I'm sure they see that all the time."

They rounded a corner into a much busier hallway filled with nurses and patients. They ducked back and into the closest unmarked door they could find. It was some sort of storage room, full of wire shelves stacked high with linens. "Why don't I just go tell them who I am and ask if I can see my father?" asked Harper.

"You heard what The Skidmarked child said," replied Nana Josephine-Ethelinda. "They are looking for you, and think your father may have something to do with your disappearance. They may not be so willing to let you see him."

"Maybe we can use these scrubs as a disguise?" asked Brian, who had already gone through most of the racks and picked out appropriate-sizes. He had actually been hoping for syringes or scalpels or something else he could use as a weapon since Harper had a big old gun and all.

"How did you do that so fast?" asked Theolina.

"I'm very good at rooting through stuff to find important things," replied Brian, beaming. "My mom drags me to lots of yard sales and rummage sales and makes me look through the piles to find socks and underwear in her size."

The others cringed, but Brian had no idea why. "I'm also an expert at unwrapping all the Christmas presents and re-wrapping them without damaging the paper, so I can find out what I'm getting without my parents knowing. They're not so appreciative about that one."

Skidmark already had his shirt and pants off and was pulling on some green pants that were a leg's length too long for him before Ethelinda could stop him.

"That's not going to work," she said. "You don't look like a medical professional."

"What do you mean?" asked Brian, struggling to pull a matching green top over his head.

"You look like a Brussel sprout," said Harper, who was two heads taller than Skidmark and about as big around as his leg.

Skidmark looked down at himself, suspecting that was some sort of insult. He pulled a mask up over his face. "I'm a visiting surgeon," he said.

"From Munchkinland? Seriously, you look like a Gummi Bear."

A few minutes later, they emerged from the store room with the two elder women dressed in scrubs and the two kids in wheelchairs, being pushed in front of them. Harper had her rifle awkwardly wedged between her legs under a blanket.

"I still say we should be pushing the old ladies," grumbled Skidmark.

"They have a lot of eight-year-old orderlies here?" replied Harper.

"We could be visiting our grannies! And I'm twelve, just like you!"

"I don't know who's more annoying, you or Pius."

"Shhh…" whispered Nana Josephine-Ethelinda as they passed a couple of nurses who gave them a strange look. They passed a few more people as they rolled through the hospital, a few more who gave them odd looks, but no one stopped them or said anything.

"Maybe we should have used the Skiddy-Boy's suggestion," said Theolina. "Probably would have been less suspicious."

"I told you," grumbled Skidmark. "You've been locked in a nursing home for years, what do you know about sneaking around?"

Theolina smiled. "How do you think I always get extra desserts, if not stealing them from the kitchen when no one's looking?"

"Right on," smiled Brian. He kinda liked the crazy old hag. Even if she had kidnapped him and cut off Keith's ear.

They turned a corner and saw a uniformed police officer sitting in a chair outside a patient's door. The old women pulled the kids back.

"Is that my dad's room?" Harper asked. "Why would they have a guard on the door?"

"Is your dad a murderous sociopath?" asked Skidmark. Harper glared at him. "What? I mean, he did drive you guys off a cliff, didn't he?"

"Maybe they're keeping someone away from him," said Theolina softly.

Before Harper could claw his eyes out, which is exactly what Brian was watching her prepare to do, the two old ladies glided down the hall and started speaking to the cop. Brian didn't catch what they were saying, but suddenly they were all gone.

"Did they just use some kind of disappearing spell?" asked Brian.

A moment later, the two women emerged from the room and waved at the kids to come join them.

"No, they just killed him," said Harper.

"We didn't kill him, he'll be fine," said Ethelinda as they approached the door.

"Mostly," added Theolina.

The old women ushered them into a small, private hospital room with no windows. The lighting was very dim, but in the centre of the room, Dick Jeddore lay in a bed and was plugged into numerous machines, wires and tubes running in every direction. An oxygen machine hissed steadily in-and-out like Darth Vader, and little electronic beeping sounds went off at regular intervals like a bomb counting down the seconds. Or someone playing the most boring game of Pong ever. Harper gasped.

"Oh my God. Dad?"

She approached him and cautiously put her hand on his arm. His dark eyes fluttered open behind his oxygen mask. They took a moment to focus, but once they settled on Harper, his bruised face smiled.

"Harper! You're okay! Where have you been, I was worried sick."

"It appears he worried so hard his spleen fell out," said Brian, trying to take in all the hoses and bandages. "The kids fell off the cliff, and they were way better off than you."

Harper leaned in to hug her father, and their embrace lasted a long time, punctuated by tears. "Dad, we have to get out of here. The Psycho Hose Beast is out there, it's looking for you."

"I know," said Dick. "Or at least, I suspected. Which is all the more reason you shouldn't be with me. You should get as far away from me as possible."

"My papa was very loving and protective as well," said Theolina, "But I must confer with your daughter. We need to keep you alive."

Dick looked at the two women, his face like Brian's parents when he tried to explain the Dark Phoenix saga to them. "Who are you?"

"Theolina Benoit," said Theolina, with a slight flourish, which was made all the creepier by the blood stains on her face and track suit. "This is my sister, Ethelinda."

Dick looked back and forth between the two women, looking more and more confused. "You're Josephine Whillet. I know you, you're Barbara O'Neill's mother."

"It's a long story," Harper sighed. "And we still haven't made much sense of it."

"Niall and Pius went to the police station for help."

"The boys are okay, too?" Dick was visibly relieved. "Thank God."

"Well except for Keith Doucette," said Brian. "Theolina cut his ear off."

"What?"

"He's a right little shit, that one," said Theolina. Ethelinda and Harper nodded in agreement.

"Oh he's not so bad," said Brian. "He likes good movies."

The beige phone on Dick's bedside table began to ring. He looked shocked and confused. "Wait, what happened to the constable that was outside the door?"

"Don't you worry your pretty little head about that." Theolina patted him on the hand. He pulled away in disgust.

Slowly, Dick reached over and picked up the phone receiver. As he did so, Brian heard Ethelinda mutter to her "sister," "He kind of looks like papa, don't he?"

Dick gingerly put the receiver to his ear. "Hello?" he said tentatively. "Sergeant Tanguay? No, I don't know where Constable Squires is or why he's not answering... Yes, they're here with me... What do you mean we have to get out right now?"

Dick pulled the phone receiver away from his head. "It's dead," he said.

A moment later, all the lights in the hospital went out, plunging them into darkness.

## CHAPTER TWENTY-FIVE

*The Skin Game*

August 23, 7:15am

"I should be telling your parents you're safe," Sergeant Tanguay said for the millionth time.

"If you do, they're going to want to know where we are," Niall reminded her. "And that will make it a lot more complicated for you to find out what's going on."

Niall had realized on the car ride over here that the Sergeant wanted to know the secret about the creature and the Benoit sisters just as much as the rest of them did. It was insane for her to be taking them with her instead of contacting their parents. She was obsessed with getting to the bottom of this, focussed to the point she was making otherwise questionable decisions. He had been using that knowledge to his advantage every time she suggested sending them home.

"Well, have you found it yet?" she asked, looking over her shoulder.

They were in a quiet corner of the empty town library, but she still seemed worried someone was going to come after the kids. The library wasn't open yet, but the librarian had quickly let them in when the Sergeant showed her badge. Pius had somehow known that the librarian, Mrs. Aucoin, would be here two hours before the place opened.

Pius was pouring over a microfiche machine. He had perked up on the drive over when he started talking about looking up information on the old women, but once he stepped foot in the library, he seemed to become a new person; the catatonic freak from the tunnels completely gone. Keith was at another table looking at magazines.

"No, it's not here," Pius moaned. "They've got a lousy selection of newspapers. Excuse me, Mrs. Aucoin?"

The librarian came back over to the desk. She was a sour old woman with blue hair who always dressed in what appeared to be furniture upholstery. "Yes Pius, my dear?"

Mrs. Aucoin hated most children, except Pius, who was always so polite and eager to talk about books. She must also never watch TV, listen to the radio or read a newspaper, or have any friends, because she didn't seem to know that Pius and the other boys had been missing. "Do you have any St. John's Telegram, from like, the 1920s?"

"Heavens no," she laughed. "We don't have the budget for that. They have them in the St. John's Library, though. I know the librarian out there, he usually starts early, too. Want me to call him?"

Niall had once asked Mrs. Aucoin to help him find a book for a school report and she had told him to not be so lazy and look it up himself. And to stop being so loud. Now here she was offering to make a long-distance call for Pius to bother another librarian during off-hours. Niall was wondering if he would have to start asking Pius for tips about women.

"We need to find anything you can about Ethelinda and Theolina Benoit," said Pius.

"I assume this is urgent?" Mrs. Aucoin asked, finally seeming to notice the blood stains on the kids, not to mention the cop standing with them.

"Yes ma'am," said the Sergeant.

As the librarian went off to make her call, the others turned back to Pius. "Okay so what else you got, kid?" asked the Sergeant.

"We need to find out more about Niall's Nana. Find out what her connection is to the Benoit Sisters."

"She was born in Lewisporte, on November 18, 1929," said Niall. "Or at least that's what Mom always told me. How do we check that?"

"Your Nana's Anglican, right?" asked Pius, and Niall nodded. "We should call the archdiocese in St. John's and get them to check for her birth certificate. See if it checks out."

"Won't that take time?"

"Not if I do it," said Tanguay, reaching for her radio.

While they were waiting for answers to come in, the boys sat nervously staring at the shelves of books. Niall always liked the library. He preferred books by R.A. Salvatore and David Eddings, though he was starting to get into Steven King. Harper really like Tolkien. Niall had never managed to get through the *Lord of the Rings*, he found it kinda boring, but maybe he would have to try it again.

"November 18, 1929?" said Pius. "Does that sound familiar?"

"Date of the Newfoundland Tidal Wave," said Keith, who they were not even aware was paying attention. "What?" he asked when he realized the other boys were staring at him. "I know stuff, even if it ain't from books. My grandfather always went on about how he and his father tied up their boat on a really long anchor line, so their boat survived the rising and falling waves while all the other boats in the harbour got wrecked."

Tanguay came back with her answer first. "No record of Josephine Biddle being born in Lewisporte in 1929."

"Why would she lie about that?" asked Niall.

"Maybe she didn't know?" suggested Pius. "Maybe that's what her parents told her."

A few minutes later Mrs. Aucoin returned. "That was fast," said Pius.

Mrs. Aucoin blushed. "I think Mr. Evans at the Memorial University Library has a bit of a crush on me. We spent a long night exchanging notes back at the provincial library workers retreat in Gros Morne last year."

Niall didn't want to think about what kind of notes they were exchanging, but it was nice that Mrs. Aucoin found someone who shared her interests. Even if she was, you know, married.

She rolled out a long sheet of curled, shiny paper onto the table. "Anyway, these Benoit sisters are interesting characters. He faxed me over the clippings. He only found a short blurb about each of them, though. First was an obituary for Ethelinda Benoit. She died in Kelly's Island during the Tsunami on November 18, 1929."

"What?" asked Niall, Pius and Tanguay at the same time.

"Did it say anything else about her?" added Pius.

"Only that she was a spinster and a recluse, and that she was survived by her twin sister, Theolina."

"And what did it say about her?"

Mrs. Aucoin scrolled through the roll of paper, which they were all leaning over, even Keith. Niall noticed the blue-haired woman's nose twitching and suddenly became self-conscious. The three boys smelled really, really bad. "Theolina Benoit was arrested in 1948 for the attempted murder of William Jeddore," read Mrs. Aucoin. "She spent time in prison and the Waterford hospital before she was released and apparently disappeared."

"She disappeared because she changed her name to Kane," said Niall. He noticed his best friend staring off into space. "Pius, what's wrong?"

"Did it say why she tried to kill William Jeddore?" asked the boy, looking a little green.

"Oh that's the best part. Apparently, she wanted to use his blood in a magic ritual. She said it was to keep a devil from escaping on earth. At her trial, she ranted on about how the 'blood of the blood' had to be spilled to save us all. Can you believe it?"

"That's messed up," said Keith. "Wait, isn't Jeddore your last name, Tonto? William Jeddore related to you?"

Pius cleared his throat. "If it's the same guy, sort of. My dad's father died when he was really young. My grandmother remarried and had a second son with a man named William Jeddore."

Tanguay gasped. "And now she's in the hospital with your uncle, who is William Jeddore's son?"

Pius nodded.

"We have to go," said Tanguay.

## CHAPTER TWENTY-SIX

*Blood Makes Noise*

August 23, 8:05am

"While we would love to wait for the telephone repairman," said Theolina, "I think it would be best if we made ourselves scarce."

"He's plugged into all these machines," said Harper, gesturing to the hoses and wires. "We can't move him."

Dick Jeddore was already pulling everything off himself. "I'm okay, Harper. I'll be fine." He winced as he yanked out the IV and hoped Harper didn't notice.

Tanguay had said to get out of there. That's all he'd heard on the phone before the line went dead. Emergency lights were flickering on in the hall outside his room, and he heard concerned voices and rushing feet as staff tried to make sense of what was going on. Presumably no one had noticed that Constable Squires was missing yet. Depending on how the old women had dealt with him, there was no telling how long it would take for anyone to find him. In the chaos now would be the best time to escape.

He trusted Sergeant Tanguay. She didn't like him, sure, but that was all the more reason to trust her. If she didn't like him and he was basically under arrest and she still warned him to run away there must have been something *really* bad happening.

Dick stood up and nearly fell on his face. It was only Harper catching his arm, and that Skidmark kid breaking his fall, that kept him from totally wiping out on the floor. He felt worse than he realized.

Harper was beside herself. "It's no good, he can't even walk!"

Theolina and Mrs. Whillet gave each other a strange look, as if a whole conversation passed silently between the two women.

"Now?" Theolina asked. "Here?"

"It's not ideal, but we could make it work," replied Mrs. Whillet.

"What are you talking about?" asked Harper.

"Your father should lay back down," said Mrs. Whillet, smiling. Dick didn't like that smile. It looked like the same one he had given Harper when he took her dog to the vet to have it put down, but told her everything was going to be okay.

"You know that thing is coming, right?" said Skidmark. "The Psycho Hose Beast that Harper shot five times and won't die? The thing that you said you were trying to protect Mr. Jeddore from?"

Dick shook his head. "Harper, you shot what five times?"

"The old underwater witch lady."

"With what?"

"Your .22 rifle," she said, sheepishly, and nodded to the weapon which they had snuck into the room and now stood leaning by the door. "I'm sorry Dad, I was trying to protect everyone."

Dick was in disbelief, but he put his hand on his daughter's black hair. Her hair looked just like Dick's mother's hair, when she was young. Harper's mother's hair was fiery red. His daughter had faced that thing and tried to kill it? While he was laying here in a hospital bed? His heart sank. He should have been out there protecting her, not making her fend for herself like that. "You shot it five times with a .22 rifle, and it kept coming?"

"Well, it fell down," she admitted. "But it kept getting back up."

"It was friggin' sick," agreed Skidmark. "It was like *The Terminator*. Or *Friday the 13th*. But again, my other point still stands: We came in here to get Mr. Jeddore out, and now you're saying he should stay here."

"We only needed to keep Mr. Jeddore safe until we had time to do the ritual," said Mrs. Whillet, and Dick felt icy fingers suddenly crawl up his spine. *The ritual?*

Theolina must have noticed Dick's apprehension. She nodded. "When we said only the 'blood of the Blood' could put the Primordial One to rest, we meant literally that we needed his blood."

She pointed an old, bony finger at Dick.

The icy fingers grabbed a hold of Dick's guts and he turned into full-on panic. He prided himself on staying pretty cool in stressful situations, but this was getting a bit too weird. "You need my blood?"

"You are the son of William, son of Richard, son of Joseph, son of Noel, son of Peter, son of Richard, son of John..."

Dick's mind was reeling. She knew his father's name, and his father's father, and his grandfather's father... after that Dick didn't even know their names himself. How did she know? She was still going back, listing relative after relative he'd never heard of. Who the hell was this woman? Could this be for real?

"...son of Wowkwis, son of Muwin..."

Wait, those weren't even names anymore, were they? They sounded familiar, though, like old Micmac words his grandmother sometimes used, that he had assumed she had made up...

"How far back are you going?"

Theolina stopped, seemingly insulted by being interrupted. She sighed and continued. "All the way to Kluskap, the First Hunter. It was by his blood that the Primordial One was originally sealed away beneath the sea, five score and four *sahasra chandrodayam* before the birth of Christ."

"Okay, that just sounded like gibberish," admitted Dick.

Theolina shrugged. "It is roughly ten thousand years ago."

"Ten thousand years?" Dick was gobsmacked. "That thing running around out there killing people is ten thousand years old?"

"Heavens, no," said Mrs. Whillet. "It is literally as old as the Earth itself. It was *imprisoned* for ten thousand years, and to be blunt, it's pretty pissed off about it."

"We slowed it down, sixty years ago," added Theolina, "when it first escaped its prison. But we did not have the blood of the Blood to defeat it completely. Now we do."

"It knows what you are," said Mrs. Whillet. "It can smell you. It is drawn to you, and will keep coming to you until it can kill you. It knows you are the best, and probably only, chance we have of defeating it."

Somewhere close by, they heard a crack of thunder. The walls of the hospital shook.

"And it's coming pretty soon," added Skidmark, who was standing by the door. "I just saw lightning flash down the hall."

It was insane. It was all madness. Ten thousand-year-old monsters and magic rituals, it sounded like something out of one of those books Pius read, the ones that Harper made fun of him for but Dick knew that she read, too. He shouldn't believe these crazy old women—especially since he knew Mrs. Whillet, had spoken to her a handful of times, and never known her to act or sound like this—but he did believe them. He had seen the creature himself, this Primordial

One, this Psycho Hose Beast. He had felt its presence and knew it was hunting him. Not just because he was alive, but because it was looking for him, specifically.

He looked at Harper, standing next to his bed, tears leaving light brown streaks through the dirt caked on her cheeks. She was looking at him for answers, to fix all of this. He was her father. That was his job. To protect her and make the world make sense. But nothing made sense anymore. He couldn't take her hand and tell her everything would be alright like when she broke her arm, or when Lucky had got hit by a car and Dick took her on what he knew would be a one-way ride to the vet. There were things in this world beyond comprehension. It was unbelievable, yet he believed.

And if he was blood of the Blood, then that meant that Harper was, too. And if he died, then she would be next on the monster's list.

She had been through so much. And he couldn't protect her from this hospital bed.

Or maybe he could.

"How much blood do you need?" asked Dick.

## CHAPTER TWENTY-SEVEN

*Sin*

August 23, 8:15am

People were streaming out of the hospital when Marie-Ann pulled her cruiser up at the front door, sirens blaring. She still couldn't raise Squires on the radio, so she called dispatch again.

"Murphy!" she practically screamed into her receiver. "I'm in front of Sir Wilfred Grenfell Hospital, do you have anything for me?"

The response came almost immediately. "Negative, Sergeant. All phone lines to the hospital are still down, we have no idea what's going on in there."

"What about my backup?"

"The next closest patrol car is still a couple of minutes away."

The people streaming out of the hospital were panicked and terrified. Some of them looked bewildered, like they had seen the depths of the hell and could never believe in goodness and truth again. She couldn't wait.

"Dammit, you stay in the car!"

She turned to the three boys in the backseat, all of them wide-eyed.

"But my uncle Dick is in there!" Pius complained.

"But Harper is in there!" said Niall.

"These doors don't open from the inside anyway," said Keith, fumbling with the door handle.

She didn't wait for any further comment. Tanguay hopped out of the car, checked her sidearm, then went to the trunk to retrieve her bullet-proof vest and shotgun. A few people came up to her asking for help or just answers, but she pushed them aside and warned them to get as far away from the hospital as possible.

Weapons ready, she took a deep breath and stepped into the front door of the hospital.

Tanguay had only once before geared up like this to walk into a dangerous situation. She had been stationed in a small town in New Brunswick when she'd gotten a call that a couple of drunks had locked themselves in their barn. They shot at anything that came near and dared the police to come try and get them. She had actually managed to get through that situation without firing a shot. In fact, only one firearm had been discharged during that stand-off, when one of the drunks accidentally shot the other one in the face when they carelessly dropped their weapons. He had lived, for better or for worse, and would spend the rest of his life with one eye and a significant portion of his skull missing as a reminder of his stupidity. That one had been a win, in Marie-Ann's books.

She doubted this one would end as cleanly.

The Sergeant headed for Dick Jeddore's room, and as she approached she found two more bodies. One appeared to be a nurse, torn open like she had fallen on a table saw, and the other was a man in maintenance coveralls, lying face down, soaking wet and bloated like he'd just been pulled out of a body of water. She didn't need to check to know that it was saltwater.

Tanguay assumed the bodies meant she was going in the right direction, but she wondered about the logic of going in alone, without backup.

She knew the creature was in here. She also knew Theolina Benoit was in here, who despite being ninety years old was possibly almost as dangerous. And she had no idea what to expect from Josephine Whillet, or why she was helping the crazy old gypsy woman. But Dick Jeddore, his daughter and that weird kid named Skidmark, were all in serious danger, and so she had no other choice.

Tanguay turned the corner and saw it. The Psycho Hose Beast, clawing at the door to Dick Jeddore's room, less than ten metres down the corridor in front of her. But it wasn't a creature. It was a woman. A terrifying woman, with red eyes and animal-like claws, dressed in ragged old clothes with stringy black hair, but she was definitely a woman. A young woman, at that. The witness reports said that she had looked old, nearly desiccated, but this woman was probably younger than Tanguay.

She looked an awful lot like Theolina Benoit, too. She could have been the granddaughter of the old woman in the picture the seniors' home had provided. Or the daughter of the woman in the grainy picture from the old newspaper she'd seen at the library.

Or the sister of the woman who had lived through the Newfoundland Tsunami, if she had stopped ageing in 1929.

The woman was pounding on the door and squealing an inhuman howl, trying to get into the room. Jeddore, and probably the others, had to be in here, and so far, she hadn't noticed the sergeant was here. Marie-Ann raised her shotgun. She was a pretty good shot, and at this distance, could take the woman's head off. She was unarmed, sure, so it might be difficult to explain to her superiors, but this might be the best chance she had of stopping it. Her. Whatever it was.

Of course, if it really was as hard to kill as the kids claimed...

Marie-Ann slowed her breathing, telling herself that even a zombie from the bottom of the ocean couldn't survive having its head blown off. She took careful aim and squeezed the trigger...

"Sergeant Tanguay!" her radio crackled to life on her shoulder. "We found Josephine Whillet's birth certificate. She was born on Kelly's Island—"

Marie-Ann didn't hear the rest of it. The woman was rushing toward her and the sergeant fired, but missed. She was moving too fast. How could anything move that fast?

She tried to fire again but her arms felt like lead. She couldn't get the gun up fast enough. It was like the black-haired woman was moving faster than an Olympic sprinter, but she was flailing underwater. What the hell was happening?

The woman leapt, her eyes burning with fire and her talon-like claws ready to claw her heart out. Marie-Ann knew she was about to die, and hoped she would see Lynne again when this was all over, but then she heard something odd that she never imagined would be the last sound she heard before shuffling off this mortal coil...

*"Informer - You no say Daddy me Snow me, I'll go blame - A licky boom-boom down..."*

# CHAPTER TWENTY-EIGHT

*Into the Fire*

August 23, 8:15am

Dick looked up at the two old women standing over him muttering words he didn't understand, and he thought that perhaps this wasn't such a good idea after all.

Theolina held a knife in her hand—a long, thin knife like the kind used by workers in a fish plant to scale fish. She said that because he was giving them the blood willingly, they wouldn't need as much, but with the tip of the blade hovering just over his eyes, that reassurance wasn't very... reassuring. It didn't help that Harper was at the foot of the bed, trembling and weeping in horror.

She was about to watch her father be ritualistically murdered by a pair of crazy old witches. This was a terrible idea...

Something heavy hit the door. It was locked, but the kid Skidmark leaned against it anyway, and his body seemed to jump when whatever was on the side slammed into it again.

"Little help here!" cried Skidmark. "It's coming!"

Harper rushed to the door and to help the other kid, and Dick felt the slightest twinge of relief. Sure, he was still going to be stabbed to death any second, but at least his kid wouldn't get a front-row seat.

Why was he doing this anyway? He wanted to help, a part of him knew he had to, but was getting stabbed the only way to do this? He couldn't run or fight, but maybe he could provide some other kind of moral support, like solving a puzzle or something? He was pretty good at crosswords.

The pounding on the door grew more incessant, and the old women's murmurings grew faster and more frantic. What were they doing? Were they rushing? He hoped they didn't screw it up and turn him into a goat or something…

Mrs. Whillet picked up his right hand and held it over his heart. Theolina slowly brought down the blade, and Dick found himself holding his breath. This was it. The moment when they revealed their true colours and turned him into cod guts sloughing off the side of the wharf into the bay.

The old woman touched the blade to the back of his hand, and Dick felt the sting of metal cutting flesh. It was just the slightest prick, and a few drops of his blood ran down the edge of the blade. The two women suddenly became quiet, holding even their breath, and for a second Dick wondered if their hearts had stopped. It felt like his had.

But nothing happened. The pounding continued outside the door.

"It didn't work…" Mrs. Whillet hissed. "Why didn't it work?"

"Maybe we need more blood?" suggested Theolina.

Before Dick could protest, there was a screech out in the hallway. The banging and scratching stopped, and Skidmark immediately unlocked the door and yanked it open.

"Not again!" screamed Harper.

Skidmark stepped out into the hallway just as a gunshot blared outside the room. It sounded like a shotgun. Everything was happening so fast—had someone shot the kid? No, he was still moving, and singing? Why was he singing? But that didn't sound like real words...

And suddenly the creature flashed by the doorway and Skidmark was gone. He screamed, once, and then there was another gunshot and the creature howled and twisted and tried to climb into the hospital room.

Then it grabbed Harper.

"Dad!" she screamed, and then was gone, dragged away by the Psycho Hose Beast, out of the room, down the hallway into the darkness.

Dick struggled to get out of bed. His head was spinning, his legs felt like they weighed a million kilograms, and his stomach threatened to turn itself inside out with every step. It took everything he had to walk across his small hospital room to the door, but he had to. He had to get to Harper.

Before he even reached the door, Marie-Ann Tanguay appeared in the opening, carrying a shotgun. The other kids, Pius and Niall and another boy Dick didn't recognize were with her. The third boy, whose head was covered in bloody bandages, was holding a black handgun.

"That was quite a shot," said Tanguay to the kid. "Wait, is that my gun? And how the hell did you get out of the car?"

"What?" asked the kid, handing the weapon back to her. "Did you think that was my first time breaking out of the back of a cop car?"

Tanguay holstered the sidearm and turned toward Dick.

"It took Harper," was all Dick could manage, but didn't need anymore. She nodded and disappeared down the hall.

Skidmark was laying on the floor in the hallway. He was hurt, but he was alive. He was groaning and trying to sit up. "She really doesn't like that song," he muttered.

Behind him in the room, Dick heard the two old women arguing over why their spell didn't work. They were talking about phases of the moon and thaumaturgic inversions and other ridiculous crap he had never heard of, until Mrs. Whillet gasped and started muttering, "Oh, no, no," to herself over and over again.

Pius and Niall were checking on Skidmark when the Sergeant re-appeared in the doorway.

"They disappeared," Tanguay said. "I followed them down to the basement and they were just gone."

"The tunnels," said Skidmark, weakly. "They went out through the secret tunnels."

"Sergeant Tanguay!" Pius and Niall said almost simultaneously, falling over themselves to get their words out. "We figured it out!"

"Figured what out?" groaned Dick. If there were secret tunnels here, they had to follow them to find Harper...

"Niall's Nana was born on November 18, 1929 in Kelly's Island," explained Pius, excitedly. "The same day and place that Ethelinda Benoit died, the same day they sisters said they banished the Psycho Hose Beast!"

"What the hell are you talking about?" asked Dick. His head hurt so bad.

"What if, when Ethelinda died, her spirit, or her soul or whatever you call it, somehow entered the baby Josephine Biddle?" Pius sounded like he was describing the plot of one of his books.

"So Nana has had two souls inside her all this time," added Niall. "The stuff she was talking about as she got older and her mind starting to go—they weren't memories of her own youth, they were memories of Ethelinda Benoit's youth. How else would she have known those things?"

"Kids, we don't have time," said Tanguay.

Pius ignored her and kept going. "And what if, when Ethelinda's soul left her body, another being that was close by—say, an immortal monster from the dawn of time—somehow got transferred into it."

"This is insane," said the Sergeant.

"No, this is exactly right," corrected Theolina, appearing in the doorway. "And explains part of the reason why our banishing spell won't work. The Primordial One is living inside my sister's body. The rituals I've been using won't work against my own flesh and blood."

"You said *part* of the reason?" asked Pius.

Mrs. Whillet—Ethelinda—sighed. "I can't perform my part of the ritual at all. The most powerful magic requires a pure mind and body. My original body had never known the pleasures of the flesh, but this one..." she gestured at her old, track-suit wearing self.

"You can't do the ritual because Nana Josephine isn't a virgin?" asked Pius. Keith snickered.

"That's exactly what I'm saying," said Mrs. Whillet.

"We still have to go get Harper!" yelled Dick, with as much strength as he could muster. All this stuff about magic and virgins didn't matter. His daughter was out there somewhere with a monster.

"Didn't you hear?" asked Theolina. "We can't stop it. Your guns are useless against it, as is our magic. It will continue drawing life from its victims until it consumes the whole world..."

Pius had a strange look on his face. Dick had seen that look before, when he had asked the kid about his science project. He looked at Theolina. "Your magic won't work because the monster shares your physical flesh." He turned to Mrs. Whillet. "And your magic won't work because your body isn't pure. But what if we had someone who was of your flesh—Mrs. Whillet's flesh, descended from her body and soul—and still pure?"

"What are you—?" Theolina started, but stopped herself. She smiled. She glanced at Mrs. Whillet, who also smiled and nodded.

Everyone looked at Niall. Everyone, even Dick, who barely knew what was going on, and even Skidmark, who was barely conscious.

"Why are you staring at me?" Niall asked.

Keith laughed. "So dork, are you still a virgin or what?"

# CHAPTER TWENTY-NINE

*Enter Sandman*

August 23, 8:25am

Fortunately Niall didn't have to answer the question. Sergeant Tanguay interjected before he could open his mouth, though Niall was sure everyone could tell his response from the redness of his face. "Keith, can you carry Skidmark out of here? I'm sorry kid, I don't know your real name."

"It's okay," said Skidmark, feebly. "Even Father Hickey calls me Skidmark."

"I carried Tonto all the way up out of the stupid tunnels," grumbled Keith. "Is that all I am? A dork delivery system?"

The Sergeant raised a finger in his face. "One, stop calling him Tonto. Do you even know who that is?"

Keith shrugged. "Buck Rogers' partner or something? I dunno, it's something my dad says."

The Sergeant ignored him and raised a second finger. "Two, if we survive this, do you want to have the local RCMP officer on your side, or looking for every possible excuse and opportunity to bust you?"

Keith, who was always getting into trouble for roughing up other kids, didn't really have much of a choice. He nodded.

"Great, take Pius too. Get outside. There are doctors there. The rest of us are going to look for Harper and the creature."

"Even me?" asked Niall, dreading the answer.

"Yeah, I'd rather take the kid that can shoot, but apparently we need Virgin Mary. You can push the wheelchair."

It was bad enough coming from Keith, but from the police sergeant, too? "You know I'm only twelve, right?"

The wheelchair she referred to was one commandeered to transport Dick, who while lucid was still in no shape to walk. It was pretty shocking that he had jumped out of the truck but was way worse off than the three kids who had stayed inside it all the way to the bottom.

On their way down the dark halls toward the basement stairs, Theolina tried to grill Niall on the proper words to use for the ritual. Niall didn't even get one in ten of them correct.

"Theolina, leave him be," scolded Nana Josephine. "We don't have time to teach him ancient Aramaic."

Niall didn't think he would ever get used to another woman's voice coming out of Nana's mouth, but at least she was still standing up for him like she used to.

"Besides, the words aren't important. They are just there to focus the mind. It's the intention behind the words that matters. What you want them, and the spell, to do. Words are meaningless and forgettable, it's the action that's the key."

"Isn't that a Depeche Mode song?" Niall asked. All three women looked at him sideways. "Nevermind," he added.

They reached the old boiler room, which was pitch-black besides their two small flashlights. Niall noticed Theolina's light, the same one she'd had since the bunker, was growing dim. At least Sergeant Tanguay's light seemed to have fresh batteries. He saw movement in every shadowy corner and hoped it was just mice or rats. They had to work their way over a pile of broken, mouldy wood, through the old secret door that led into the tunnels. It fell to Niall to heave the wheelchair over the wreckage while Sergeant Tanguay covered the door with her shotgun. As he hefted chunks of wood out of the way, watching the two old women and the half-dead man in the wheelchair, Niall was struck by the sudden realization that if anything happened to the cop or she was otherwise indisposed, he was the fittest member of their crew. Between this and the fact that Theolina was still trying to teach him Aramaic did not bode well for their mission.

The going was much easier in the tunnels proper, with Dick's wheelchair moving easy enough over the mostly-level floors outside an occasional crack or small pile of broken concrete. As they travelled with the Sergeant on point, the two old women continued to grill Niall on what he had to do. "You have to imagine it," Nana kept saying. "You have to picture pushing the Primordial One away, as far away as you can. To the moon, if you can picture it clear enough."

"Not far enough," growled Theolina. "Push that bastard all the way back to the dawn of time. Make it regret ever crawling out of the pus-filled boils of Mother Earth."

Niall had no idea what she was talking about and certainly couldn't picture it. He thought maybe he could manage the moon. After watching it fifty-plus times on video, he could also perfectly picture Gotham City from Tim Burton's *Batman*, but Niall figured that probably wouldn't work. Seeing as how it was fictional and all. And yet this unkillable monster from the abyss was somehow real.

"Theolina will be there," Nana reminded him, though whether it was for Niall's benefit or the old women's, he wasn't sure. Theolina seemed to be getting more irrational the deeper they went into the tunnels if that was even possible. She kept talking about doing obscene things to the creature that Niall was pretty sure his twelve-year-old ears weren't supposed to hear. Nana shook her head and placed her hand on Niall's shoulder. It felt odd. It wasn't something Nana usually did. "She will guide you. You just have to work with her. Only together will you be able to truly banish the creature."

"There!" Dick said, so abruptly that Niall stopped in his tracks and nearly dumped the injured man out of the wheelchair. He was pointing at something on the ground. They had come to an intersection in the tunnel, and somehow Dick had noticed some sign of which way their quarry had gone. Niall hadn't even realized he was watching for tracks, though to be fair he was a bit distracted on wondering how he was going to exorcise an otherworldly demon.

Sergeant Tanguay knelt down and checked the floor. She nodded, apparently agreeing with Dick's assessment of the situation. "This way," she said and hurried off down the right corridor without really waiting for Niall and the old ladies to keep up.

"She knows we're ninety years old, right?" Theolina groaned as she shuffled after the cop.

"You're ninety," Nana reminded her. "Technically, this body is only in its sixties, though she hasn't kept very good care of it. What does this body eat, Niall?"

Niall shrugged. "Nana does have a soft spot for Central Dairies ice cream."

A scream up ahead in the darkness indicated they were indeed going the right way.

"That was Harper!" Dick cried, and Niall instinctively found himself running in the direction of the scream. His heart had dropped below his stomach all the way to his shoes. There was no way they were going to reach her in time.

Sergeant Tanguay was sprinting full out now, and very quickly disappeared ahead of them. "Marie-Ann!" Dick called out. "Marie-Ann, do you see her?"

There was no response. Niall ran for a couple of minutes until his breathing became too laboured and he had to slow down. They were in total darkness now, and he had no idea where they were going. The cop had run off with one flashlight ahead of them, and the other one was with the old ladies, who had now fallen behind.

"What do we do?" Niall asked. Now his heart was coming back up, but it sailed past his chest and stuck in his throat.

"Keep going!" Dick growled. "We've got to get to Harper!"

Niall wanted to say that if they made it to Harper and the Psycho Hose Beast, without Theolina, there was no way they could combat her. But the words wouldn't come out. He wanted to get to her, too. He didn't really believe he could somehow do magic on the monster anyway. But maybe they could save Harper.

He only got a few steps before they heard another scream, this one behind them. And it wasn't Harper's voice, but that of a much older woman.

"It's behind us," Dick said, though Niall didn't need the words to know what was happening. It had circled behind them somehow. He also didn't need any suggestions on what to do this time. He turned the wheelchair around and started running back in the direction of the scream. He had no idea if the scream belonged to Nana or Theolina, but either option was too horrible to consider. If it was Nana, that meant the monster was killing the woman who helped raise him. If it was Theolina, then that meant it was killing the one person who may be able to stop it.

They were almost back and could see the vague shadows of legs illuminated by the dropped flashlight up ahead when a sudden, blinding burst of blue light flashed through the tunnel. Niall and Dick both howled and Niall stumbled backward. Dick spilled out of his chair.

It was the same lightning they had seen over the harbour, the upside-down lightning from when the creature had killed those two fishermen. The same lightning Skidmark said he saw when his neighbour died.

His vision blurred and spotted, Niall crawled toward the shadows. There was one woman lying on the floor of the tunnel, and another pressed up against the wall, with what could only be the Psycho Hose Beast crouched over her. When he had first seen the monster, it had been decayed and falling apart. But now it's healing had progressed so far that it passed beyond a normal, healthy human into something else entirely. Its flesh was too plump, like overripe fruit about to burst. Veins actually pulsed through its thick, elongated arms with too much blood and fluid. Its fingers and claws were longer, its face was swollen up like a hideous balloon, smoothing out its features so the eyes were only two tiny red pinpricks hidden deep in folds of bulbous flesh. Its yellow teeth were obscured by distended purple lips

Nana was screaming, and the creature looked like it was about to devour her face. Theolina Benoit lay drowned and dead beside her.

"No!" Niall screamed, without thinking, the sound escaping his lips nearly as fast as Pius telling on him when he stole a box of Oreo cookies from the cupboard. What was he going to do now? Theolina was the only one who could help him banish the creature, wasn't she?

It looked up. It saw Niall and Dick Jeddore and its hideous face twisted in what could only be a smile. Either that or it smelled something really, really heinous. It took two steps toward them, and then the creature's head exploded.

The shotgun blast left his ears ringing, but Niall didn't care. The Psycho Hose Beast hit the ground, over half of its swollen head splattered on the wall of the tunnel. Was that it? Was that all it took to kill the thing?

No. It was still moving, trying to stand up, even without a head.

Sergeant Tanguay came up behind them with Harper in tow. She shoved Niall aside, pulled Nana to her feet and yelled at all of them to get away. Niall could barely hear her over the ringing in his ears. The cop unloaded twice more into the creature, blasting it in a gooey mess, and for a split second, Niall thought that maybe it would work this time. But then it started to crawl toward them again, and Tanguay just ushered them all down the corridor, pushing Dick's wheelchair herself this time.

# CHAPTER THIRTY

*Superman's Song*

August 23, 8:50am

They got lost in the tunnels. They just ran, hurrying as fast as they could, but they could hear the weird moans of the creature following them. The RCMP officer's flashlight darted wildly back and forth as they went, making their travel as nauseating as it was terrifying.

"How is it moaning?" Tanguay groaned, oblivious to her unsteady light-work. "I blew it's friggin' head off!"

"Obviously it grew back, duh," said Harper, running close by her father's side.

They burst through an open steel door into a small chamber and found themselves at a dead end.

"What is this?" asked Dick. "This doesn't look like the rest of the tunnels."

The room was only three metres across, so it was cramped with all of them in it. The walls and floor were metal, studded with heavy metal rivets. The air inside was even cooler than the other tunnels. Opposite the door they entered, there appeared to be another door, with a small round window in it. Tanguay peered into the window and gasped. "*Tabernack...* are we... underwater?"

"We're under the Bay," Dick said, himself in shock. "I didn't realize we came so far."

"Is this an airlock?" asked Harper.

"It has to be," answered Niall. "Part of the old American base. All of these tunnels were. But what the hell were they doing here?"

Tanguay, exploring their surroundings, shouldered her shotgun and grabbed the open door they'd come through. It barely moved. "Kids, help me close this."

Harper and Niall jumped into action, and Niall gasped as soon as he put his shoulder against the cold metal door. It felt like that time he had helped his father push their car off the road when they broke down, but he'd accidentally left it in park. The door weighed a ton and was grinding against decades of neglect. It was moving, just very, very slowly.

"I don't know if that's going to work," said Nana.

"It's thirty-centimetre-thick steel," replied Tanguay. "It will keep it out."

"I still don't think it will work," Nana said, grimly.

They had the door over half-way closed when the Psycho Hose Beast's arm reached through and grasped Harper by the hair. Niall let go of the door and grabbed Harper, trying to pull her away. The creature's grip was unshakeable.

Tanguay brought up her shotgun to fire just as the monster's bulbous head started to squeeze through the opening. It released the girl and grabbed the gun instead, snatching it so hard that it yanked the cop face-first into the steel door. The collision of her skull and the metal made a sickening thud, and Tanguay dropped her weapon. She slunk to her knees.

The creature started to squeeze the rest of its body through the gap. Niall saw its head push through like Play-Doh being forced through one of those plunger-shapes, followed by its other arm. It was now grasping and clawing into the airlock, leaving long gashes in the steel with its talons.

There was nowhere to go. They were trapped in this tin can with this unstoppable creature that was going to devour all of them.

Suddenly, thick hands grabbed the creature's forearms and pulled it forcefully all the way into the airlock. "Get out!" Dick Jeddore screamed. "Get out!"

Harper and Niall were stunned, but fortunately, Nana was alert enough to shove the children through the open door, which was just barely wide enough for all of them to fit through. The old woman followed.

Through the small gap in the door, Niall could see Mr. Jeddore wrestling with the Psycho Hose Beast. He was pinning it to the floor with his wheelchair, and Niall could see his arms trembling from the strain and his rapidly-failing strength. It was amazing he could hold it back at all, even temporarily; the monster must have been severely weakened by the shotgun wounds.

"Dad!" Harper screamed and reached for the opening, but Nana held her back. Niall grabbed her, too, far too shocked at the moment to even notice he had inadvertently brushed her boob.

The scream seemed to bring Sergeant Tanguay around. She staggered to her feet, her unfocused eyes dancing between the door and Mr. Jeddore. As her senses returned, she started to look around the small room, searching for her gun.

"Go!" Mr. Jeddore screamed at her. The creature was getting free. "Get the kids out of here!"

The cop hesitated for a fraction of a second, but when Mr. Jeddore said "kids," she seemed to make up her mind, darting through the narrow gap. She really had to squeeze to make it through in her bullet-proof vest, but the second she was clear she started pulling the big wheel from the outside, trying to close it. It moved, but barely.

"Help!" Tanguay screamed, as the creature shoved Mr. Jeddore aside and turned it's red eyes to the door. "Help me!"

Niall dove to the door and helped her pull. It moved another couple of centimetres, but it wasn't moving fast enough. The tunnel was dark, but Tanguay had dropped her flashlight inside the airlock, illuminating it in long shadows. The creature was crawling across the floor, Niall could just see it out of the edge of the porthole in the outer door. It wasn't even remotely human anymore. The thing had been blown apart and rebuilt so many times it was now just a mass of bone, blood and swollen, puffy flesh dressed in tattered rags. It was more like some sort of insect with a freakish, Cabbage Patch Doll-like head. And very long, skinny arms that could easily reach through the small gap of the door...

Niall knew they weren't going to make it. They should give up and run, but he knew there was no escaping this thing. Guns couldn't stop it, the old witch was dead... it was going to keep coming until it killed them and everyone else. He pulled for all he was worth, his arms and back straining with more pain than he had ever felt. He heard Sergeant Tanguay screaming beside him, the veins in her neck and head threatening to explode. But still the creature drew closer and closer, it's long, black, bloody claws reaching for the tiny open gap...

There was an awful bang as something hit the door and it slammed closed, plunging them into darkness but for a murky glow coming from the small porthole window. Niall was knocked backwards onto his butt, but he looked up and for a split second they saw Dick

Jeddore's face in the porthole. He was bruised, and bloody, but he was smiling. His eyes, full of tears, met Harper's for just a moment, and he was smiling.

And then he was gone, and they heard terrible, muffled crunching sounds inside the airlock.

Nana covered Harper's face and held her close. The girl was screaming and sobbing. Sergeant Tanguay turned the wheel to lock and seal the airlock. She glanced into the window but quickly averted her eyes, took a moment to steady herself, then slid to the floor against the cool concrete wall, exhausted.

"Now what?" Niall asked. He couldn't bring himself to look at Harper. His heart and stomach felt like they'd been turned inside out, and he didn't know what to say or do.

"Just give me a minute," Tanguay said softly, trying to catch her breath. "Then we'll go get a truckload of dynamite and blow this bastard to Kingdom Come."

"How many times do we have to tell you, you can't kill it like that," said Nana, her arms still clutched around Harper.

"We have to destroy it," said Harper through gritted teeth. "Open the airlock and drown it under the sea."

Nana shook her head. "It survived under the Atlantic for eons in its original form, and for another sixty years in my body. It will not die. And this cage will not hold it."

They all jumped as an ear-splitting, metal-shearing squeal roared from inside the airlock. Tanguay leapt up and looked through the porthole again. "It's trying to claw itself out!"

Niall felt his knees grow weak. They couldn't do this. There was no escape. Their only hope had been the witches and Mr. Jeddore's blood, and now both of them were gone...

"Niall, you have to do it," said Nana.

It took him a moment to realize she was talking to him. "What?" Niall asked.

"You have to banish it. You have a piece of my body and soul in you. You can do the ritual."

"I can't... I can't do magic. I needed Ms. Kane to do it, you said so yourself. I can't even say the stupid words."

"You don't need the words. You don't need anything special. All you need is the intention. Think about sending the creature away. Far away, as far as possible. Think about that as hard as you can."

This was stupid. "I can't..."

"You have to. Or we all die."

She sounded like Nana then, for just a second. Like her voice, anyway. But Nana had never said anything so chilling. Niall felt his stomach twist and freeze. If he'd eaten anything in the last two days, it would have come back up.

"But what about... you said we needed Mr. Jeddore's blood..."

Harper stood up. Her dirty face was still streaked with tears, but her mouth was firmly set. She pulled her pocket knife from her jeans and without hesitation, snapped open the blade and ran it across her hand. She didn't even flinch as small droplets of blood began to drip down her palm and her wrist.

She extended her hand to Niall. "Do it."

With trembling fingers, Niall took her hand. Her blood was warm and sticky between their palms. He could feel her heartbeat through her fingers. He always dreamed of holding her hand, but it had never been like this. Never with her blood dripping between his fingers and a monster trying to kill him and he somehow about to try to banish it to another world.

Still, her hand felt good. With all the other madness and horror they'd seen, even if they died in the next few minutes, at least he got to hold her hand. Sure, he would die a virgin, but that was the only way he was able to do this spell, anyway.

Niall reached out with his free hand and touched the porthole. He didn't look at the monster but instead closed his eyes. He could see it well enough in his mind. The image of that thing would haunt him for the rest of his life, even if that life was as short as he was expecting. He focused on that image, and the feel of Harper's heartbeat in his hand and blocked out everything else. He ignored the screeching metal. Ignored his own racing heart, which felt like it was going to explode like that time the AC adapter on his Nintendo melted and burst after he left it on for 30 hours straight. For some reason, he couldn't ignore the ocean though, which he felt particularly strongly. It was above and all around him, an unfathomable weight and power, a power far greater than anything he had experienced. It should have made him afraid, but it didn't. He should have been terrified that all that stood between them and the crushing, cold Atlantic was 50-year-old steel and concrete, but he felt more peaceful than he ever had in his life. The sea gave him comfort. And he knew what he had to do. He could see the Psycho Hose Beast so clearly in his mind's eye.

*It took the sea an hour one night...*

But really, all it needed was a second.

"Go away," Niall said quietly, and the creature was gone.

*Niall found himself standing on a cliff, overlooking the crashing ocean below. He wasn't in Gale Harbour, and this wasn't St. Stephen's Bay. He didn't recognize the shoreline.*

*It was dark and overcast, but he couldn't tell what time of day it was. There was a dim, diffuse glow coming from somewhere, but whether it was the sun or moon filtering through the clouds was impossible to say. The only light coming from the small, old-*

*fashioned houses a few hundred metres down the shore appeared to be oil lamps or candles.*

*The ocean was shockingly calm, and still. Niall had grown up within walking distance to the ocean and had never seen the sea so perfectly smooth. Not a single wave rippled upon the black, featureless surface. It looked like an endless plane of glass.*

*He suddenly realized two women were standing near him. He didn't know them, but he did recognize them. They both looked identical, which was some combination of the Primordial One's human form and a much younger version of Theolina.*

*"Thank you," said the first sister. Her eyes were brown and pretty. Full of life. Her hair was nearly as black as the sea below. "You finally set me free."*

*Niall opened his mouth, then closed it again. He tried to think of something cool to say, but everything sounded dumb in his head. Finally, he just went with the truth. "I don't know what I did."*

*The sisters laughed. "None of us ever do," said the other one. "We just do our best, to help the ones we love." She took her sister's hand, and their fingers intertwined. "Sometimes we're right, and sometimes we're wrong."*

*"Sometimes we cock-up completely," added the first one. "But we're never really wrong if we're true, and do what we know is good in our heart."*

*Suddenly the women's voices grew muffled, and they suddenly seemed farther away. Niall panicked slightly, as the edges of the world around him became dull and blurry.*

*"It's up to you, now, Niall. Take care of her."*

*Niall was being pulled away from them now at a breakneck pace. The sisters were becoming just a tiny speck on the horizon. But he had so many questions for them...*

*"Who?" Niall asked. "Take care of who?"*

*But they were already gone.*

When Niall awoke on the floor of the tunnel a few moments later, he was nauseous and disoriented. It was impossibly dark, the only light coming from the tiny flickering flame in the corner of his vision. It took him a moment to remember where he was. He finally sat up to see the stunned faces of Harper and Sergeant Tanguay staring at him. The Sergeant was holding a small cigarette lighter.

"What happened?" he asked. His voice felt weak and his throat scratchy, like that time he and Pius had screamed Guns-n-Roses and Metallica songs at the top of their lungs for three hours.

"You did it," Harper said. She was smiling, but there was still sadness in her eyes. There was something else, too. Fear, maybe? Definitely uncertainty. But she held out her hand and helped Niall to his feet. He felt something when their fingers touched, different than the last time, and not just because of the dried blood on her palms.

She pointed to the steel door, and Niall peered through the porthole. He couldn't see anything at first—the flashlight must have gone out. But as his eyes adjusted, he saw something moving through the gloom.

A fish swam by, just in front of his face.

The airlock was full of water. Had they opened the door on the other side? No, he couldn't see the other door or even the wall on the far side of the chamber. All he could see was water and the murky bottom of St. Stephen's Bay until it blurred away into inky nothing. He could just make out the broken twisted metal edges of the floor and ceiling where the entire outer wall of the airlock had been completely torn away.

"You don't remember?" Harper asked, seeing the shock and confusion on his face. "You just blasted it away. Poof! The creature, the airlock, everything was just shredded to dust in a heartbeat, and the water rushed in and washed it all away."

"I don't... I don't know what I did."

Harper shrugged. "Nope. After it happened you just kinda turned toward us and went, 'Did I do thaaat?'" and then passed out. She quoted him in a nasally, high-pitched voice that was far more Steve Urkel than Niall actually sounded (at least he hoped it was).

A split second later, Niall remembered who else had been in that airlock, and what he had done to ensure the rest of them survived. Harper must have seen his realization because when he met her eyes, she shook her head and pointedly looked away. Before he had to say anything, their awkward moment was interrupted by soft groans.

A few metres away, Sergeant Tanguay was kneeling next to Nana, who also appeared to be coming around as if she had been asleep.

"What's wrong with her?" Niall asked, going to his grandmother's other side.

"She passed out at the same time you did," explained the cop. "I don't think she hurt herself when she fell, but give her some air, she may be disoriented..."

Nana's eyes darted around the dimly-lit tunnel, fear and confusion washing over her. She looked like she did that time Niall and his mother found her a few weeks ago, wandering around her neighbourhood without any pants on. That had been one of the final inciting incidents to put her in the nursing home.

"Niall, where am I?" Nana asked, her eyes fixing on her grandson.

Niall felt his heart jump. "Nana, you know who I am?"

"Of course I do, where the devil are we?"

There was something about Nana's eyes. They were far more alert and knowing than Niall had seen them in a long time. They were also back to their natural grey colour, unlike the brown they had been when Ethelinda was driving.

"Ma'am, do you know who I am?" asked Sergeant Tanguay.

Nana looked her up and down strangely. "I guess you're a Mountie, but I don't think we've ever met."

Tanguay and Niall glanced at each other. So had she forgotten everything else from the last few days?"

"Nana, do you know where you are?" Niall asked.

"Not the foggiest. Some sort of basement or something? Niall, I'm getting upset, what's going on?"

Tanguay took a deep breath. "Everything is okay, ma'am, everything is perfectly fine. You are safe, and so is Niall, we all are. But please tell me, do you know who you are? Where and when you were born?"

"That's foolishness, of course I know who I am. I'm Josephine Whillet, I was born in Lewisporte on November 18, 1929."

Niall released a deep sigh. He looked down and realized he was still holding Harper's hand. She was holding on extremely tight, and Niall saw she was still on the verge of tears. She wouldn't meet his gaze, or anyone else's. He might have been relieved to have gotten through this with his grandmother intact, but Harper had not been so lucky. He could not fathom what she was going through. He squeezed her hand back as tightly as he could. He smiled, despite himself, but it came from a painful place.

Nana looked at him sideways. "What's so funny?"

"I have no idea. And actually, Nana, you weren't born in Lewisporte, you were born in a little community called Kelly's Island. We've got a lot to talk about..."

## CHAPTER THIRTY-ONE

*Come As You Are*

September 7, 1992, 1:30pm

Pius and Niall were sitting on Pius' patio in his backyard on a sunny Labour Day afternoon. They were playing *Double Dragon II* on their cable-linked Game Boys, taking advantage of the sunlight to see the dim and usually nigh-invisible screens.

School was supposed to start tomorrow, but it was postponed as the town dealt with the aftermath of the storm and the multiple deaths it had caused. Most of the deaths had been blamed on the storm, though Niall still couldn't figure how or why the RCMP insisted on covering it up. He supposed people better knew how to cope with the destruction caused by merciless weather than by elder gods from another dimension.

There had been a few of the deaths, of course, that couldn't be explained away by drowning or being exposed to the elements. Those were blamed on an elderly woman named Kane who suffered from dementia, who had escaped the senior's home and went on a rampage. That had been the part that the media caught onto, and everyone seemed to accept that story and gleefully reported on it, even if all the facts didn't quite add up. It bothered Niall that Theolina would be remembered as a psychotic killer when in fact she had given her life trying to save everyone in Gale Harbour, but honestly, he suspected the crazy old woman would have gotten a kick out of it.

A few metres away from them, on the grass under a tall maple tree, Harper sat reading a book. She had come to live with Pius' family, as no one had been able to track down her mother. Pius' parents didn't want to get her involved anyway and said they would do everything they could to sort out the legalities to make sure Harper could stay with them permanently. Harper seemed to agree with them, though she hadn't spoken much since the day in the airlock. She spent most of her time, whenever it was daylight and the sky was clear, sitting in Pius' yard, reading.

"Maybe I should go talk to her," said Niall, pausing the game and looking up.

"Leave her be," replied Pius. "My mom tries to talk to her all the time and she barely says a word. My dad says she's not ready yet."

Niall watched her, sadly. He hadn't spoken to anyone much, either. He had only told his parents that they had been lost in the woods and were trapped in a bunker for a few days. They knew he had a run-in with the "Psycho Hose Beast," but they thought he meant Ms. Kane. He hadn't shared any specific details. Without really discussing it in advance, Pius had told his parents basically the same thing, so their stories matched up. For some reason, none of them really wanted to share what had happened. Except for Skidmark. Apparently he had told his parents everything, then they had beaten him for lying and making up horrific stories.

They had been through so much together, they could possibly be the only ones who could understand. Niall wanted to talk to Harper, maybe they could help each other, but only she had experienced such a deep, personal loss, and Niall was afraid to approach her because of it. He felt like anything he said to her couldn't possibly even begin to deal with what she had experienced, so he said nothing.

Niall and Pius returned to their game but were only playing for a few moments when two other boys entered the yard. A few weeks ago Niall would have been shocked to see the two of them together, but now nothing surprised him.

Skidmark and Keith approached them, both carrying backpacks. Skidmark, with one arm in a sling and the other leaning on a crutch for support, was dressed in dirty old grey sweats. Keith wore a brand-new Vuarnet t-shirt and Umbro soccer shorts, but both boys were wearing identical Toronto Blue Jays baseball caps. Keith's was oddly lopsided due to his bandaged ear.

"What's up, boys?" asked Keith, and Niall instinctively flinched. Usually, a greeting from Keith Doucette was followed up by a sucker punch to the gut, but this time he seemed genuinely cheerful.

"Why is he here?" Pius moaned, shifting on the patio's bench seat so he was slightly behind Niall.

"I know what you're thinking," said Skidmark, holding up his good hand and nearly losing his balance as soon as he let go of the crutch. The hand was covered with something brown and sticky, presumably remnants of the Fudgsicle that was melting all over the cast on his other hand. "And normally, I too would be apprehensive about an unannounced Keith Doucette entering my property bearing gifts."

"It's like a Trojan Horse full of dipwad," said Harper, who had approached the patio as well, probably to protect Niall and Pius from the bully.

"Now, hear him out," said Skidmark. "I was skeptical, but his offer is surprisingly enticing and relatively low on the potential for physical harm."

Niall nearly burst out laughing. Compared to last week, juggling chainsaws was relatively low on the potential for physical harm.

"Look, boys," said Keith, imploring. "I know you don't like me much, and I get that. I can be a right ass sometimes. But I just needs someone I can hang out with and talk to about this stuff."

Niall actually felt bad. Of course, the poor guy felt just as lost and alone as the rest of them did. He had also seen stuff no kid their age should have to deal with.

Keith shrugged his backpack off and started opening it. "And I know you guys aren't exactly into stealing your folks' booze or racing dirt bikes or playing hockey..."

"Those are probably the three lowest things on my to-do list, yes," agreed Niall.

"Eh, only bottom five, for me," said Skidmark.

"...but I got something here that you might be into. My brother left these when he went away to university. I don't really understand it, but it looks a lot like the *Final Fantasy* games, which are pretty cool. My brother raved about it, though my mother said it was all Satanic crap."

Keith threw a stack of hardcover books on the patio. Niall, Pius and Harper leaned in close to look. The top book showed a knight with a winged helmet riding a horse and wielding a big-ass sword.

"*Advanced Dungeons & Dragons, Second Edition?*" read Pius.

"You want to play Dungeons & Dragons with us?" Niall asked.

"Yeah, sure," said Keith. "Might be cool, right? It comes with all these weird coloured dice."

"I've already got ideas for a campaign," said Skidmark.

Pius and Niall looked at each other and shrugged. They had actually talked about playing a few times, but neither of their parents would ever let them get the books. Their moms would let them read Stephen King books about sex and gore and worse, but they both saw that Tom Hanks movie back in the eighties and now both were convinced Dungeons & Dragons was the devil.

"Screw it, we're in," said Niall, and Pius nodded.

They each grabbed books and started to flip through, but Niall stopped. It wasn't the walls of text and confusing charts and sexy pictures of half-naked warrior women that stopped him. He realized that Harper had started walking back to her tree with her book, apparently satisfied that Keith was no longer a threat. But that didn't sit well with Niall. She was part of this, too. And hey, she said she liked Ralph Bakshi movies, and he had seen David Eddings and Tolkien books on the shelf at her dad's place...

"Hey, Harper," Niall called out. "Wanna play with us?"

Harper stopped. Niall noticed her black hair glowed in the sunlight like polished stone. She turned and glared at Keith. "Did you break Suzie Fowlow's arm?"

Niall winced. Harper was known to hold a grudge, and to be fair, that was a pretty serious offence. Niall suddenly felt dirty, having forgotten about it himself.

Keith shook his head. "I swear to God, I did not. We were arguing at the Lion's Club playground, and she fell off the monkey bars. I never laid a hand on her. I tried to help but she told me to screw off. Next day she started telling people I broke her arm. Not many people wanted to believe me over her, you know?"

"You are known to be a right butt monkey," agreed Pius. Everyone stared at the small boy, dumbfounded.

"What's this?" Keith grumbled. "Little Pius suddenly starts cracking wise?"

"You like it?" asked Pius.

"No, not really," replied Keith. Everyone else agreed. Pius was always supposed to be the nice one.

Niall looked over to Harper and was surprised to find her smiling. "Fine, I'll play your dumb game. As long as I don't have to wear a dorky cape or anything."

"Capes?" asked Keith. "Do we have to wear capes?"

Harper walked over and joined them on the patio, and picked up a copy of *The Monstrous Manual*. She sat down next to Niall and continued to smile.

Craig Muise swept his flashlight beam back and forth across the grey concrete floor and wall of the tunnel as he and his buddy, Scott Legge, crept slowly through the dark labyrinth under Gale Harbour.

Craig was dressed in a heavy winter coat and wet boots, his Ski-Doo branded toque pulled down over his ears. His mitts were tucked into his coat pocket and his fingers were freezing, but it was the only way he could turn the pages of the graph-paper notebook he was carrying. He scribbled notes with his pencil.

They came to a fork in the tunnel, and Craig consulted his hand-drawn map. He and Scott had been mapping these passages for three months, ever since the secret tunnels became common knowledge. Technically it was illegal to enter the tunnels, and all the known entrances were sealed off, but once everyone knew they were there it didn't take long for alternative entrances to pop up. Everyone in town was shocked that these had existed for nearly fifty years and no one knew about them. Everyone except Old Gussy Shave that is, who lived in his fishing shack out in Port Hansen. He had apparently been talking about secret passages under the town for years, but everyone just figured he was crazy. He also said that Elvis was alive and hiding out in Keeping, so he probably was actually crazy; he just happened to be right about the tunnels.

"I'm telling you," Scott was rambling on as Craig tried to get his bearings. "I played this new arcade game on the ferry to Nova Scotia. It's called *Mortal Kombat*—Kombat with a K, for some reason—and it's friggin' awesome. It knocks the pants off *Street Fighter*, I'm telling you."

"Nothing beats *Street Fighter*," replied Craig, his eyes still locked on the map. He looked up and flashed his light down the left-hand fork in the tunnel. He was pretty sure they hadn't explored that way yet.

"No, seriously, I'm telling you—it's got blood and it looks super-realistic and you can punch a dude's head off and everything. It's totally wicked."

Craig, who usually just ignored Scott, and usually only kept him around for company in the dark, spooky tunnels, finally looked at his friend. Scott was the same age as Craig but puberty had hit him hard. He had stretched out like a sickly weed and to say his acne-ridden face looked like pizza would have been unfair to pizza. But his smile— missing several teeth from hockey games earlier this season—was infectious. "Seriously?" asked Craig. "You can punch a dude's head off?"

"I'm telling you, it's awesome. And there's this ninja guy who stabs you with a spear, like 'Get over here!' and blood sprays everywhere. It's supposed to be coming out for the Super Nintendo and Genesis later this year."

"Huh," said Craig, genuinely intrigued. "I'll have to check that out." He turned back to the tunnel, pulled on his mitts, and headed down the new, unexplored passage. Scott continued to ramble on about *Mortal Kombat,* or maybe he was talking about a Jean Claude van Damme movie now, Craig wasn't really paying attention.

The new tunnel didn't go far before ending in another rusted metal door. Finding doors down here wasn't unusual; there were plenty of them separating what appeared to be old offices and storage rooms, as well as access to ladders and stairs leading up to the surface. But this one was different because it was the first one Craig encountered that was locked.

It also featured a faded yellow sign with red letters that read: *Caution: Restricted Area—Authorized Personnel Only.*

A heavy-duty but very old padlock sealed the door shut. Craig gave it a couple of yanks with his gloved hand and it felt pretty solid. If *Goldilocks and the Three Little Bears* had taught him anything as a kid, it was that he should probably leave well enough alone. But they had already come this far. And everyone knew a sign saying, "Do not enter," was the best way to make someone actually want to enter. It was like a restaurant where you couldn't get a reservation—it made everyone want to get a reservation.

"Give me the crowbar," said Craig, holding out his hand.

Scott slipped his bag off his shoulders and produced a long, steel pry bar. "You sure? Isn't this like, breaking and entering?"

They had carried the crowbar after encountering a few doors that had been stuck with rust and age, but this would be the first time they actively had to break into somewhere. "We're already breaking and entering."

"But it says 'Restricted Area.' What if, like, John F. Kennedy's brain is in there or something?"

Craig rolled his eyes. He wedged the crowbar between the lock and the pin and started to push. "This place has been sealed off for forty years. It's probably just old mouldy files or something. But what if it is something cool? Don't you want to see it?"

Scott only had to think about it for about a second and a half before he grabbed the bar and helped Craig push. With the two of them, it only took a moment to pop the lock off, and the door opened surprisingly easy after that.

Craig's flashlight beam fell upon the room inside, which was a little bigger than the other storerooms they'd found, maybe five metres square or so. Except this one, unlike the others, wasn't empty.

In the centre was a large, fat, cylindrical object about a metre thick and three metres long, covered in a dusty old tarp.

Craig and Scott looked at each other, shrugged, then approached the object together, and yanked off the tarp in a cloud of dust that made both boys choke and cough.

When the dirt settled, the boys found themselves staring at a huge, green bomb-shaped metal device, pocked with rust and covered with faded "Danger" warnings and "Radioactive" symbols.

"Is... that what I think it is?" asked Scott.

"Holy shit," breathed Craig.

## About the Author

C.D. Gallant-King is a writer, tabletop gamer, pro-wrestling aficionado, father and husband. He was born and raised in a town that looks suspiciously like Gale Harbour, and currently resides in Ottawa, Ontario, Canada. Find out more at www.cdgallantking.ca

## Other Books by C.D. Gallant-King
*Ten Thousand Days*
*Hell Comes to Hogtown*

## The Werebear vs Landopus Series
*Tentacles Under a Full Moon*
*Revenge of the Lycanterrancephalopod*
*The Gun Nun*

Printed in Poland
by Amazon Fulfillment
Poland Sp. z o.o., Wrocław

62761033R00150